THE NEW WINDMILL BOOK OF

STORIES FROM AROUND THE WORLD

EDITED BY HILARY PATEL

Heinemann
New Windmills

Heinemann Educational Publishers
Halley Court, Jordan Hill, Oxford OX2 8EJ
a division of Reed Educational & Professional Publishing Ltd

OXFORD   MELBOURNE   AUCKLAND
JOHANNESBURG   BLANTYRE   GABORONE
IBADAN   PORTSMOUTH (NH) USA   CHICAGO

04 03 02 01 00
13 12 11 10 9 8 7 6 5 4

ISBN 0 435 12480 3

Acknowledgements
The editor and publisher wish to thank Siân Chafer for her assistance in checking the construction
of the activities, and the following for permission to use copyright material:
Laura Cecil for 'How Table Mountain Got Its Cloth' from *An Eye for Colour* by Norman Silver, page
9; Hilary Patel for 'Beneath the Baobab' from *Passport Magazine*, 1992,,page 23; Aitken & Stone
Ltd. on behalf of Shiva Naipaul for 'Mr Sookhoo and the Carol Singers' included in *A Man of
Mystery and Other Stories*, Penguin Twentieth-Century Classics, 1995, page 47; Sheil Land
Associates Ltd on behalf of R.K. Narayan for 'Cat Within' from *Malguidi Days*, 1982, page 62;
Heinemann Publishers Oxford for 'The Martyr' from *Secret Lives* by Ngugi wa Thiong'o, page 73;
Anya Sitaram for 'Naukar' from *Flaming Spirit* published by Virago Press, 1994, page 85; Mrs
Althea Selvon for 'A Drink of Water' by Samuel Selvon, page 101; Heinemann Publishers Oxford
for 'Looking for a Rain God' from *The Collector of Treasures* by Bessie Head, page 112; Random
House UK Ltd for 'Country Lovers' from *Soldier's Embrace* by Nadine Gordimer, published by
Jonathan Cape Ltd 1980, page 117; Seema Jena for 'The Bamboo Blind' from *Flaming Spirit*
published by Virago Press, 1994, page 128; David Higham Associates Ltd on behalf of Alice
Walker for 'Everyday Use' from *In Love and Trouble* published by The Women's Press, page 137;
Ruth Cohen Inc. on behalf of Lensey Namioka for 'The All-American Slurp' copyright © 1987 by
Lensey Namioka, from *Visions* edited by Donald R. Gallo. All rights reserved by the author, page
149; Peter Owen Ltd for 'The Empty Amulet' by Paul Bowles, page 161; *Critical Quarterly Magazine*
for 'Mondi' by Claire Macquet, 1989, page 167; Jonathan Clowes Ltd on behalf of Doris Lessing for
'A Sunrise on the Veld' from *This was the Old Chief's Country*, copyright, © 1951 by Doris Lessing,
page 179.
Whilst every effort has been made to locate the owners of copyright, in some cases this has been
unsuccessful. The publishers apologize for any infringement or failure to acknowledge the original
sources and will be glad to include any necessary corrections in subsequent printings.

Cover painting 'Mata Mua (in olden times)' by Paul Gauguin reproduced
by kind permission of Art Resource, New York.

Cover design by The Point
Typeset by Books Unlimited (Nottm) NG19 7QZ
Printed and bound in the United Kingdom by Clays Ltd, St Ives plc

Contents

Introduction

Short stories have existed for a very long time. The written story is perhaps better known today, but there was a time when stories were told or sung in the form of folk tales, myths, legends, fables and parables.

Writing down stories has advantages and disadvantages. The main advantage, of course, is that the written story is saved for ever from being lost or forgotten, as many of the old oral stories must have been. The disadvantage is that it becomes fixed in form and wording, and something valuable is lost in the process. A story recited from memory is uniquely different each time it is told. It might be told by a different story-teller, or the story-teller may have adapted their tale according to mood and to suit a particular audience. They may have missed out parts of the story or added new parts, varying the tone and presentation. These oral stories which live in people's memories are as adaptable in the telling as the people themselves. They have a lasting freshness and direct appeal to the listener which can easily be lost when they are 'frozen' in print.

No story was ever told or written simply so that it might be 'learned'. The primary purpose of story-telling is to give pleasure. Stories may do this in a number of ways – by the reader's enjoyment of a clever plot, by being well-written, by causing pleasant associations, by creating suspense or stimulating anticipation or reflection. They may give pleasure, too, by increasing the reader's understanding and appreciation not only of the stories themselves but of the culture in which they are rooted. This, in turn, can give the reader a new understanding through comparison and reflection of the reader's own circumstances and experiences.

The oral tradition still survives in many of the countries from which the stories in this book are taken although it is gradually giving way to the written word, and its survival is evident in many of these 'stories from around the world'. Through them we can gain a valuable insight into the cultures and traditions of other people, whose countries we may never visit. They are a 'window' into other worlds which also casts light upon our own.

Earl Lovelace, the celebrated writer from Trinidad and Tobago, once wrote: 'Nobody is born into the world. Every one of us is born into a place in the world, in a culture, and it is from the standpoint of that culture that we contribute to the world.' * No country has a single culture – each has many cultures which do not confine themselves to national boundaries. So, although many different countries are represented in this selection of stories, it is important to appreciate that countries count less than cultures and that, within cultures, there are individuals who count most of all.

Unlike novels, which are concerned with extended action, short stories usually focus on a specific event. They concentrate on examining how individuals respond to a limited situation. These responses will be conditioned by the culture in which the individual is living, which has its own rituals, beliefs, peculiarities and customs. Therefore, each story asks us to consider people's responses to the unique and particular set of conditions in which they live.

* *Wasafiri* No 1 Autumn 1984

On the other hand, although the physical environment and cultural framework may be different from our own, human beings throughout the world experience the same range of emotions. Jealousy, fear, elation, rage, grief, guilt, hope, happiness and the great themes of love, death and change are common to human experience. It isn't always necessary to be familiar with a culture in order to understand what is happening in a story. There will always be individuals whose characteristics we can recognize and identify with, and as the stories are read people will understand them within the framework of their own personal experiences. So, although there are differences between cultures, there are also enough similarities for us to recognize the universality of human nature. We might even agree, as Chief Kinombwe suggests in *Beneath the Baobab*, that 'we are not so different after all, though our customs and traditions would have us believe otherwise'.

Hilary Patel

Liliana Heker *was born in Argentina in 1943. She won the Casa de las Americas Prize for fiction at the age of 23 with her book of short stories,* Los que vieron la zarza (Those Who Beheld the Burning Bush). *Liliana continued to write in Argentina during the military dictatorship of the seventies, despite serious dangers and difficulties.*

Norman Silver *was born in Cape Town, South Africa in 1946. In 1969 when he came to England to study, the cultural differences he experienced caused him to review his ideas, most especially about South African racial thinking.*

The children in the following stories realize that things are not always as they seem. Basil in How Table Mountain Got Its Cloth *learns that there are two sides to the legend of Table Mountain, depending on what colour you are. He also learns more about Dolly's boyfriend, Floyd. In* Stolen Party, *Rosaura experiences dejection at the end of a party which earlier had made her feel that 'she had never been so happy in all her life'.*

The Stolen Party

Liliana Heker

As soon as she arrived she went straight to the kitchen to see if the monkey was there. It was: what a relief! She wouldn't have liked to admit that her mother had been right. *Monkeys at a birthday?* her mother had sneered. *Get away with you, believing any nonsense you're told!* She was cross, but not because of the monkey, the girl thought; it's just because of the party.

'I don't like you going,' she told her. 'It's a rich people's party.'

'Rich people go to Heaven too,' said the girl, who studied religion at school.

'Get away with Heaven,' said the mother. 'The problem with you, young lady, is that you like to fart higher than your ass.'

The girl didn't approve of the way her mother spoke. She was barely nine, and one of the best in her class.

'I'm going because I've been invited,' she said. 'And I've been invited because Luciana is my friend. So there.'

'Ah yes, your friend,' her mother grumbled. She paused. 'Listen, Rosaura,' she said at last. 'That one's not your friend. You know what you are to them? The maid's daughter, that's what.'

Rosaura blinked hard: she wasn't going to cry. Then she yelled: 'Shut up! You know nothing about being friends!'

Every afternoon she used to go to Luciana's house and they would both finish their homework while Rosaura's mother did the cleaning. They had their tea in the kitchen and they told each other secrets. Rosaura loved everything in the big house, and she also loved the people who lived there.

'I'm going because it will be the most lovely party in the whole world, Luciana told me it would. There will be a magician, and he will bring a monkey and everything.'

The mother swung around to take a good look at her child, and pompously put her hands on her hips.

'Monkeys at a birthday?' she said. 'Get away with you, believing any nonsense you're told!'

Rosaura was deeply offended. She thought it unfair of her mother to accuse other people of being liars simply because they were rich. Rosaura too wanted to be rich, of course. If one day she managed to live in a beautiful palace, would her mother stop loving her? She felt very sad. She wanted to go to that party more than anything else in the world.

'I'll die if I don't go,' she whispered, almost without moving her lips.

And she wasn't sure whether she had been heard, but on the morning of the party she discovered that her mother had starched her Christmas dress. And in the afternoon, after washing her hair, her mother rinsed it in apple vinegar so that it would be all nice and shiny. Before going out, Rosaura admired herself in the mirror, with her white dress and glossy hair, and thought she looked terribly pretty.

Señora Ines also seemed to notice. As soon as she saw her, she said: 'How lovely you look today, Rosaura.'

Rosaura gave her starched skirt a slight toss with her hands and walked into the party with a firm step. She said hello to Luciana and asked about the monkey. Luciana put on a secretive look and whispered into Rosaura's ear: 'He's in the kitchen. But don't tell anyone, because it's a surprise.'

Rosaura wanted to make sure. Carefully she entered the kitchen and there she saw it: deep in thought, inside its cage. It looked so funny that the girl stood there for a while, watching it, and later, every so often, she would slip out of the party unseen and go and admire it. Rosaura was the only one allowed into the kitchen. Señora Ines had said: 'You yes, but not the others, they're much too boisterous, they might break something.' Rosaura had never broken anything. She even managed the jug of orange juice, carrying it from the kitchen into the dining-room. She held it carefully and didn't spill a single drop. And Señora Ines had said: 'Are you sure you can manage a jug as big as that?' Of course she could manage. She wasn't a butterfingers, like the others. Like that blonde girl with the bow in her hair. As soon as she saw Rosaura, the girl with the bow had said:

'And you? Who are you?'

'I'm a friend of Luciana,' said Rosaura.

'No,' said the girl with the bow, 'you are not a friend of Luciana because I'm her cousin and I know all her friends. And I don't know you.'

'So what,' said Rosaura. 'I come here every afternoon with my mother and we do our homework together.'

'You and your mother do your homework together?' asked the girl, laughing.

'I and Luciana do our homework together,' said Rosaura, very seriously.

The girl with the bow shrugged her shoulders.

'That's not being friends,' she said. 'Do you go to school together?'

'No.'

'So where do you know her from?' said the girl, getting impatient.

Rosaura remembered her mother's words perfectly. She took a deep breath.

'I'm the daughter of the employee,' she said.

Her mother had said very clearly: 'If someone asks, you say you're the daughter of the employee; that's all.' She also told her to add: 'And proud of it.' But Rosaura thought that never in her life would she dare say something of the sort.

'What employee?' said the girl with the bow. 'Employee in a shop?'

'No,' said Rosaura angrily. 'My mother doesn't sell anything in any shop, so there.'

'So how come she's an employee?' said the girl with the bow.

Just then Señora Ines arrived saying *shh shh*, and asked Rosaura if she wouldn't mind helping serve out the hot-dogs, as she knew the house so much better than the others.

'See?' said Rosaura to the girl with the bow, and when no one was looking she kicked her in the shin.

Apart from the girl with the bow, all the others were delightful. The one she liked best was Luciana, with her golden birthday crown; and then the boys. Rosaura won the sack race, and nobody managed to catch her when they played tag. When they split into two teams to play charades, all the boys wanted her for their side. Rosaura felt she had never been so happy in all her life.

But the best was still to come. The best came after Luciana blew out the candles. First the cake. Señora Ines had asked her to help pass the cake around, and Rosaura had enjoyed the task immensely, because everyone called out to her, shouting 'Me, me!' Rosaura remembered a story in which there was a queen who had the power of life or death over her subjects. She had always loved that, having the power of life or death. To Luciana and the boys she gave the largest pieces, and to the girl with the bow she gave a slice so thin one could see through it.

After the cake came the magician, tall and bony, with a fine red cape. A true magician: he could untie handkerchiefs by blowing on them and make a chain with links that had no openings. He could guess what cards were pulled out from a pack, and the monkey was his assistant. He called the monkey 'partner'. 'Let's see here, partner,' he would say, 'Turn over a card.' And, 'Don't run away, partner: time to work now.'

The final trick was wonderful. One of the children had to hold the monkey in his arms and the magician said he would make him disappear.

'What, the boy?' they all shouted.

'No, the monkey!' shouted back the magician.

Rosaura thought that this was truly the most amusing party in the whole world.

The magician asked a small fat boy to come and help, but the small fat boy got frightened almost at once and dropped the monkey on the floor. The magician picked him up carefully, whispered something in his ear, and the monkey nodded almost as if he understood.

'You mustn't be so unmanly, my friend,' the magician said to the fat boy.

'What's unmanly?' said the fat boy.

The magician turned around as if to look for spies.

'A sissy,' said the magician. 'Go sit down.'

Then he stared at all the faces, one by one. Rosaura felt her heart tremble.

'You, with the Spanish eyes,' said the magician. And everyone saw that he was pointing at her.

She wasn't afraid. Neither holding the monkey, nor when the magician made him vanish; not even when, at the end, the magician flung his red cape over Rosaura's head and uttered a few magic words . . . and the monkey reappeared, chattering happily, in her arms. The children clapped furiously. And before Rosaura returned to her seat, the magician said:

'Thank you very much, my little countess.'

She was so pleased with the compliment that a while later, when her mother came to fetch her, that was the first thing she told her.

'I helped the magician and he said to me, '"Thank you very much, my little countess."'

It was strange because up to then Rosaura had thought that she was angry with her mother. All along Rosaura had imagined that she would say to her: 'See that the monkey wasn't a lie?' But instead she was so thrilled that she told her mother all about the wonderful magician.

Her mother tapped her on the head and said: 'So now we're a countess!'

But one could see that she was beaming.

And now they both stood in the entrance, because a moment ago Señora Ines, smiling, had said: 'Please wait here a second.'

Her mother suddenly seemed worried.

'What is it?' she asked Rosaura.

'What is what?' said Rosaura. 'It's nothing; she just wants to get the presents for those who are leaving, see?'

She pointed at the fat boy and at a girl with pigtails who were also waiting there, next to their mothers. And she explained about the presents. She knew, because she had been watching those who left before her. When one of the girls was about to leave, Señora Ines would give her a bracelet. When a boy left, Señora Ines gave him a yo-yo. Rosaura preferred the yo-yo because it sparkled, but she didn't mention that to her mother. Her mother might have said: 'So why don't you ask for one, you blockhead?' That's what her mother was like. Rosaura didn't feel like explaining that she'd be horribly ashamed to be the odd one out. Instead she said:

'I was the best-behaved at the party.'

And she said no more because Señora Ines came out into the hall with two bags, one pink and one blue.

First she went up to the fat boy, gave him a yo-yo out of the blue bag, and the fat boy left with his mother. Then she went up to the girl and gave her a bracelet out of the pink bag, and the girl with the pigtails left as well.

Finally she came up to Rosaura and her mother. She had a big smile on her face and Rosaura liked that.

Señora Ines looked down at her, then looked up at her mother, and then said something that made Rosaura proud:

'What a marvellous daughter you have, Herminia.'

For an instant, Rosaura thought that she'd give her two presents: the bracelet and the yo-yo. Señora Ines bent down as if about to look for something. Rosaura also leaned forward, stretching out her arm. But she never completed the movement.

Señora Ines didn't look in the pink bag. Nor did she look in the blue bag. Instead she rummaged in her purse. In her hand appeared two bills.

'You really and truly earned this,' she said handing them over. 'Thank you for all your help, my pet.'

Rosaura felt her arms stiffen, stick close to her body, and then she noticed her mother's hand on her shoulder. Instinctively she pressed herself against her mother's body. That was all. Except her eyes. Rosaura's eyes had a cold, clear look that fixed itself on Señora Ines's face.

Señora Ines, motionless, stood there with her hand outstretched. As if she didn't dare draw it back. As if the slightest change might shatter an infinitely delicate balance.

How Table Mountain Got Its Cloth

Norman Silver

What would most people do if they were walking along and they found a discarded handbag under a hedge and in it were a pair of diamond earrings and matching necklace?

I think what one would find most difficult in those circumstances would be to stop oneself from screaming, 'I'm rich! Thank you God almighty!' and dancing with joy in the street.

Probably what most people would do, in fact, would be to walk off with the handbag as quickly as possible – not too quickly or people might notice – until they got home. Then they could scream about newly acquired wealth to their heart's content.

The only reason I mention this situation is because that is what happened to Dolly last year.

And it shows you what kind of a person she is, because after finding the jewels, she looked through the rest of the handbag, found some plastic bank cards and a diary, and worked out who the bag belonged to and the address of its owner.

Dolly then went to that address, which was in the neighbourhood, and rang the bell.

A lady about fifty-something years old opened it.

'Excuse, Missus,' Dolly said.

'My bag!' the woman exclaimed, her cheeks flushing all colours of the rainbow, one after the other. 'Where did you find my bag! I've just notified the police! God, I thought it was gone forever! A man snatched it right off my arm in Dorchester Avenue. He cut the strap, look! My heart! My blood pressure! I nearly died when he pulled it off. But where did you find it, you wonderful girl!'

The woman checked the contents.

'Thank God, the jewellery is there. But where's my purse? You didn't see my purse? My money has been stolen.'

The woman looked like she was going to have a heart attack on the spot, but eventually she calmed down and remembered Dolly who was standing there patiently on her front doorstep.

'Wait there, my girl, you deserve something for returning this to me.'

She retreated indoors, then returned a couple of minutes later with two ten rand* notes.

'That's for you, my girl,' the woman said. 'Thank you very much.'

'Thank you, Missus,' Dolly said.

The next day, my ma read in the *Cape Times* that a Mrs Kraichik had been robbed in Bishopscourt in broad daylight. The thief had stolen her purse containing fifty rands, but ignored her earrings and matching necklace, worth over 14,000 rands. These, the article said, had been returned to Mrs Kraichik by an anonymous coloured woman, who had found the discarded bag under a hedge.

'And all she gave you, Dolly, was twenty rands,' my ma said. 'She must be a stingy old cow.'

But it shows you the kind of person that Dolly was, doesn't it, even if she had no idea at the time how valuable those jewels were.

Dolly has worked for our family seven years now, and most of that time she seemed contented, as far as

---

*   rand: unit of South African currency

I could tell. Except that she had a very low opinion of herself.

'My younger sister, Betty, she works in O.K. Bazaars as an assistant. My brother, Herman, he works in the Standard Bank on the counter. But me I'm too stupid to work in the town.'

Her only hope, she said, was to marry someone with a good job, otherwise she'd be a servant all her life.

Dolly cooked for us, and cleaned for us, for over seven years, and the only thing I ever heard her complain about was cigar and pipe ash on the carpets and the settee.

My dad always smoked cigars. How well I remember those drives all over the Peninsula with the smoke from his cigar filling the whole car. Of course, it wasn't so bad in summer, when the windows were open, but in winter, when the constant rain depressed everyone's spirits and the cold weather meant that the car windows had to be shut, it was a different proposition.

The car filled with acrid cigar smoke and my ma and Ivan and me had to put up with it the whole journey. How my dad saw out the windows to drive was beyond human understanding, because the smoke was thick, thick, thick. Talk about getting stuck in a fog, we used to carry our own fog with us, and wherever we went, it went. It was like the pillar of smoke in the Bible leading Moses through the desert, except that the smoke in our car was leading us nowhere fast and made us all so irritable that we spent the entire drive coughing, spluttering and finding the scenery miserable. Of course it was miserable – we could hardly see it because of the smoke!

But I'll say one thing for my dad. He never inhaled. He said it was bad for the lungs. The only drawback was *I* didn't know how to breathe without inhaling. So I don't suppose my lungs benefited from my dad's not inhaling.

Anyway, cigar smoke is not as bad as pipe smoke, especially if the tobacco is Springbok. I speak here from experience, because one of my dad's friends, Irving Brodie, from the house diagonally behind ours, smokes a pipe with Springbok tobacco. Ugh! As soon as he walks in the house I can smell it on him, even before he takes out his black pipe and his yellow and white pouch of Springbok tobacco.

I don't know how he manages to be director of an advertising agency. The only thing he could persuade me to do would be to keep a healthy distance between him and me. But still he keeps on trying to persuade non-whites to buy washing-up liquid, even though they've managed for years without some polluting yellow chemical in a squeezy bottle; and still he tries to persuade them to use toothpaste even though some of their teeth, especially the Africans' teeth, are far whiter and healthier than Irving Brodie's teeth which are stained yellow from tobacco.

Really, when those two get together to play chess, if possible, you should try and spend the day in Oudtshoorn. Because the room gets all murky with cigar smoke and pipe smoke and openings and endgames, and before long they are cursing each other and blaming each other for the wrong moves they made. Yet, at the end of a session, they always arrange to play again.

'That was a good game,' Irving says, 'especially the endgame.'

'No, the endgame was spoiled when you knocked over your pipe and interrupted my concentration,' my dad says. 'But next time I'll definitely beat you. It's my turn to play white.'

My ma used to get mad at them for making so much mess on the carpet and the furniture, but the next morning it was Dolly who would have to clean it all up with the vacuum cleaner.

'What for are these ashtrays?' Dolly would complain. 'They think a ashtray is a ornament!'

You know what those two guys reminded me of? Of the story of how Table Mountain* got its cloth.

I first heard that story when I was a kid. My ma was a great storyteller: every night she would tell me a different story. I don't know where my ma got all those ideas from; I suppose they just sprung up in her brain like a hot spring, but some of the stories she got from books. One of my favourites was how Table Mountain got its tablecloth.

That tablecloth must definitely be one of the seven natural wonders of the world. Every so often it gets laid there, a beautiful white cloth of clouds sitting on the flat tabletop, just as if guests were expected. The best view of it, I think, is from Bloubergstrand, looking across the bay. Even if I live to be 100 and move to the Kalahari Desert, I'll never forget that image. It's burned into my soul just like they brand cattle with a number in the movies. Also I was born halfway up the lower slopes of Table Mountain, in the Hope Nursing Home, so the first air I ever breathed was the air around that mountain.

The story of the tablecloth concerns the retired pirate, Ort van Hunks, who settled in Cape Town at the time when it was still a halfway-house on the shipping route to India. There had been nothing halfway about his pirating; he was stinking rich, so he

---

* Table Mountain: a distinctive landmark: Table Mountain has a flat top, often covered in cloud

could afford a nice farm with many strong slaves to work it for him.

His only trouble was his fat, nagging wife, who complained to him regularly that his tobacco was falling to the floor and making burnmarks on her lovely furniture. So Van Hunks had to get away from her every so often, and where he went was to this ridge between Table Mountain and Devil's Peak. There he sat smoking his clay pipe without disturbance, looking down on the fairest Cape in all the world, watching the old-fashioned sailing ships resting in the harbour.

But one time as he sat there, he was disturbed by this sudden, irritating voice.

'Morning, *meneer**! You don't mind if I join you, do you?' a little man said, doffing his hat.

'Who the hell are you?' Van Hunks asked.

'Very well put,' the intruder said, turning around to show his backside where his pointed tail protruded from a carefully tailored slit in his pantaloons.

'You're sitting on my peak,' he said, pointing to the Devil's Peak behind them, 'so I thought I'd come and join you.'

'The Devil, hey?' Van Hunks said, quite impressed. 'I thought I'd got away from the Devil by coming up here.'

The little man pulled out of his coat pocket a heavy iron pipe.

'You don't mind if I load up, do you?'

'Be my guest,' Van Hunks said, handing over his large pouch of tobacco.

The two men sat and smoked amicably, until Van Hunks produced his dice.

'Feel like a game?' he asked the Devil.

*   *meneer*: mister

'What could be better?' the Devil answered. 'Where's your money?'

Van Hunks fancied he could beat the Devil at any game, no matter what stakes they played for. He opened his bag of loot on to the rock. This loot was still left over from his pirating days. There were gold coins and silver goblets and diamond rings, some still with fingers in them.

'Is that all you've got?' the Devil asked.

'I wasn't expecting you,' Van Hunks answered.

'Oh, all right then, I'll give you credit on your soul, if necessary.'

'That won't be necessary,' Van Hunks thought to himself, knowing full well that his dice were loaded and that he could not lose.

So they started playing, and they smoked as they played, and as they played they smoked, and the more they played, the more they smoked, and the more they smoked, the more they played, until the smoke was so dense, it became difficult to see the dice. They knocked out their pipes, refilled with tobacco, and began again, smoking and playing, playing and smoking.

This is the part of the story that I get reminded of when I see my dad and Irving Brodie playing chess. The only difference is that I've never noticed either of them having a tail.

Anyhow, while they were playing, a fierce south-easterly wind blew up, and as well as giving the sailing ships in the harbour a rough time, it also blew the white smoke across the flat top of Table Mountain.

The dice game continued, with the pipes being lit again and again, until the billowing cloud completely shrouded Table Mountain.

Finally, Van Hunks excused himself.

'I must go now, otherwise that wife of mine will give me a worse hell than you could ever imagine.'

He stood up, gathering his winnings, and his pipe and tobacco.

The Devil also stood up; his tail no longer protruded from his pantaloons as it had been handed over to pay his debt.

'You must come play again,' the Devil said, 'so that I can win back my tail and also your soul.'

'Not until next summer,' Van Hunks said. 'I suffer terribly from arthritis. I never come up here in winter.'

And so it is, year after year, whenever Van Hunks and the Devil gamble with each other, that the thick cloth of smoke from their pipes covers Table Mountain.

Well, that's the story as my ma told it, and I always used to think it was a good story when I was a kid. But it was the Brodies' garden boy, Amos, who showed me that there are at least two sides to every story.

Amos has worked in the garden of that house ever since I can remember. First he worked for the Rudniks until Mrs Rudnik died. When the Brodies took over, they asked Amos to stay on, because he was so reliable and had looked after the place so well.

The Brodies had no children, or maybe they did, but they were all grown up. So why they wanted such a big place, I'll never know. They entertained a lot, and often seemed to have people staying with them, but their sparkling swimming pool and tennis court were hardly ever used.

If it wasn't for Dolly, I would never have found out this thing about Amos that really shocked me. Dolly knows everything that goes on in the neighbourhood. She and her friends can gossip for hours about what's

going on in each of the houses, with the masters and
the madams, and what's going on with the servants,
and with the garden boys, and even, I'm sure, what's
going on with the dogs and the cats. In fact she
gossiped so much that my dad once asked her if anyone
paid her for bits of gossip.

'No, Master,' she said.

'Well, I don't see why I should pay you either for
gossiping.'

That cut down her gossiping for a while, but not for
ever.

Anyway, she certainly knew what was going on with
Amos, because she had this thing going with him, even
though he had lots of Xhosa* blood in him, I think, and
she was mostly coloured. She used to spend a lot of her
off-time with him even though she had another boyfriend, Floyd, who pestered her constantly to marry
him. In fact, she had been strolling with Floyd near
Kirstenbosch Gardens, she said, when she had found
the handbag belonging to Mrs Kraichik, and it had
been on his advice that Dolly had returned the
handbag to its owner, even though she admitted the
jewels were so tempting.

'You take those and you'll get married to a jail,'
Floyd had warned her.

My young brother, Ivan, and me always used to have
this joke about Amos.

'Knock, knock!'
'Who's there?'
'Amos.'
'Amos who?'
'A mosquito.'

---

* Xhosa: tribes from the Cape district of South Africa

I don't suppose it was at all funny really, but it used to make Ivan laugh, so forever in our heads Amos became Amosquito.

'I saw Dolly holding hands with Amosquito,' I would say and Ivan's face would light up.

'Amosquito likes her, doesn't he?' Ivan would say.

'Yes, but Dolly's boyfriend, Floyd, doesn't like Amosquito,' I would say.

'Do you think Dolly will marry Floyd or Amosquito?' Ivan would say, cracking up with laughter.

So it came as quite a shock to me one day when Dolly let slip that Amos had just passed his matric. Passed his matric? God, I thought, I didn't know that Amosquito could pass even Standard 2!

'But he hasn't been going to school, Dolly,' I said.

'Night school,' she said. 'He has been going to night school for years and years.'

'Now he can get a good job and you two can get married.'

Dolly smiled coyly and looked at the ground.

'First he's going to learn correspondence,' she said.

The next time I was in the garden near the Brodies' loquat* tree that used to hang over into our garden, I watched Amos digging the vegetable garden.

He looked up at me and caught me watching him.

'Dolly says you passed matric,' I said to him. 'Congratulations!'

'Thank you, Basil,' he said. I never even knew that he knew my name.

'Dolly says that maybe you will do a correspondence course.'

'No, I'm not so sure. It took me so long to do matric in my off-time. Maybe I will do articles. I want to be a lawyer one day, if I don't get too old.'

---

*   loquat: a small yellow fruit

I looked at Amos. I suppose he was getting on, but he still wore his old brown velskoen* shoes with the laces untied, the same way he'd worn them ever since I could remember. It struck me that you could never have guessed from someone's shoes what the person who was wearing them was really like.

'You're not too old to be a lawyer,' I said.

'I hope not,' he said. 'Our people have a great need for lawyers. What are you going to study when you leave school?'

'Journalism,' I said.

'Well, it's a good job as long as you tell the bitter truth, hey! You mustn't add a sugar coating to what's going in this country.'

From that time on, I always tried to chat to Amos over the fence. He never stopped his weeding or digging while I was talking, but he seemed to enjoy my conversation and I enjoyed his, at least until the day he told me his opinion of the Van Hunks story.

It came up because he was talking about how he had been a gardener in white people's gardens for so many years.

'It's okay if it's your own garden,' he said. 'But working this hard for someone else is completely stupid. Especially for the rubbish wage *he* pays me.'

He pointed derisively towards Mr Brodie's house.

'Don't you get paid well?'

'Look at these grounds. I know every corner of grass here, and everything growing in it, and I've done all the work here, and *he* doesn't ever step outside here to even look at his own property.'

'I know what you mean,' I said. 'It's not right.'

* velskoen: shoes made of rawhide

I was proud that I could talk so easily with a non-white and vice versa, that he could talk so easily with me. Especially about his opinions of white people.

'This is such a beautiful place, man,' he said, looking up at the mountain behind him. 'This should be shared for all people.'

'I agree with you,' I said. 'But there's a lot of white people who think they own all this.'

Amos stopped for a rare instant.

'How can anyone *own* mountains or land or sky?' he said.

I didn't answer. I looked where he was pointing.

'See those clouds,' he said. 'They will soon lay the tablecloth up there. Don't you think that's one of the seven wonders of the world?'

'*Ja**,' I said. 'Old Van Hunks must be having a good smoke up there with the Devil.'

Amos looked at me like I was mad.

'I thought you knew better, Basil.'

'Knew what?'

'That Van Hunks story is a load of bulldust! You want to be a journalist, man – can't you see that it's a white man's story? They tell it to each other to make it seem that even the tablecloth on Table Mountain was made by a white man. And what's more, a corrupt white man who kept slaves to do his labour and who cheated when he played dice. That tablecloth, don't you know, used to blow up on that mountain top long before any white man ever arrived in the Cape in his little boats. It has been there since that mountain was born! Only a white man could come up with this idea that the tablecloth is only 300 years old. And only a white man would believe such nonsense. I didn't

* *Ja*: yes

expect *you* to believe it. It's a bad story anyway, because how long do you think the white man can cheat the Devil without losing his soul?'

I was taken aback by the force of his outburst. Didn't he realize that I had the power, if I wanted, to go and tell Mr Brodie everything? I could repeat Amos's words about rubbish wages and I'm sure Mr Brodie wouldn't have hesitated to fire Amos on the spot.

On the other hand, Amos obviously had a good point.

'I don't *believe* that story, Amos. I've never thought about it the way you have. But you're right. It is a white man's story. I was just referring to it as a stupid story that I was told when I was a kid.'

'Ja, well, Basil, nothing's as simple as it looks.'

I don't know who was more disappointed, Dolly or me, when Amos suddenly left his job. I suppose Dolly must have been, because her hopes of freedom vanished into thin air like a magician's trick.

Amos disappeared without saying a word to anyone. I supposed he didn't want to have an upsetting farewell scene with Dolly.

A few days afterwards, she heard that there had been one almighty argument between Mr Brodie and Amos.

'That man is terrible!' Dolly said to me. 'He found one of Amos's books and he said he would call the police if Amos didn't leave straight away.'

'Why?' I asked. 'What's so wrong about a book?'

The incident was confirmed by my ma when she bumped into Mr Brodie one day at the hypermarket.

'That's what comes of being liberal with these people!' Mr Brodie had said to her. 'It's not worth it. You give them a baby finger and they want the whole hand. Did you know that boy got his matric? A garden boy with matric! Have you ever heard of anything so ridiculous? And then he gets so big for his boots, he even reads his books while he's supposed to be working.'

Since that time, Dolly has been waiting three years for a word or something from Amos. I think she still believes that he will call for her one day like a prince in shining armour and ask her to marry him.

'Then I will start my new life,' she says.

But Amos never called for her. She heard a rumour once, though, through a cousin of a friend of hers who works in Oranjezicht, that Amos was working in the garden there for another white family.

'Maybe he will always be a gardener,' I said.

'No way,' she said. 'Not Amos. He has a ambition and he will do it, for sure.'

A few months later, she told me that she had heard from her brother that he knew a man who had been arrested during a protest march, and that he was being defended in the court-case by a new lawyer who looked like a Xhosa. And the thing that convinced her the lawyer was Amos, was that although he had shiny new black patent leather shoes, he walked about with the laces untied.

As it turned out, Dolly afterwards found it very useful to personally know of a lawyer. That was the time when Floyd was arrested and taken to court for stealing ladies' handbags.

Hilary Patel *was born in Liverpool in 1945. She lived in Zambia, where* Beneath the Baobab *is set, for twelve years.*

Victor Kelleher *was born in London in 1939. He settled in Australia, where* Footprints *is set, in 1976.*

In both of these stories the main characters find that the past takes on a new dimension beneath the roots of fallen trees. In Beneath the Baobab *it is necessary for Tyrone Brown to uproot an ancient baobab tree in order to build a road. In* Footprints *it is the wind, and not a person, which is responsible for felling a giant fig tree. But like Tyrone Brown, Benny also finds history exposed beneath the roots.*

Beneath the Baobab[*]

Hilary Patel

The village of Kinombwe rests snugly at the foot of the escarpment, out of reach of the river in spate. The villagers do not yet know that I have returned, nor that I have brought Chiti back to them.

Beyond the village, the Luapula River, spreading its tapered fingers into the sluggish swamps, flows as it did when the Portuguese and the Arabs fanned out across the continent, vying for trade routes with their caravans of copper, ivory and slaves, before consciences were tapped and the missionaries arrived; flows as it did when Nkuba of the Kinombwes killed the son of his brother Nachitu, when Nkuba fled to the swamps, and when Nkuba was found and banished.

History flows with the water and history is in all of us. The mutilation on my face is proof of that.

---

[*]   *baobab*: distinctive looking African tree, with root-like branches

The view is the same, except for the straight black scar dissecting the rich red earth and its mantle of green – the road that uprooted my destiny.

It was to help build that road that I'd come out. I, along with other expatriate development deliverers, had come to weave infrastructure into the fabric of backwardness. But the road we built did more than that: it spliced together lives which should have forever remained apart.

My forefathers had come originally from Africa: that was an irrefutable fact. Exactly from where was an unanswerable irrelevant question, I had thought. My roots had been severed long ago, and I had not come with any intention of building a bridge between past and present. Yet even so, the past was there, waiting to grasp me in its tentacles.

As an ego-booster, it would have been comforting to think that competition for the job had been stiff. But even at the time, I'd known that was not the case. It's only now I wonder: was my name written there all along? Coincidence is a tricky word. How easy it is to manoeuvre facts and call it fate. Chief Kinombwe did all that – and more.

We in the road team led an artificial life. Africa was all around us, but our contrived community isolated us from it. Us, we: the expatriates. And I was part of the 'us' and the 'we'; never 'them'.

It was fortunate, I often reflected, that this Englishman with the black skin had not come looking for a cultural liaison, since he found little of that, much more of heat, tedium and problems.

Twelve months on and the current problem was a capricious local chief declaring that a gnarled old baobab in the middle of where the final section of road should go, could not be felled – all because of some mumbo-jumbo about spirits of the dead lurking in the subterranean depths beneath the roots.

Ours was not a piddling little road – ours was a highway; a road that ran straight and a road that knew where it was going. It was a tight squeeze sometimes, fitting it in between the swamp and the escarpment, but the path of progress was uncompromising. Because of the natural obstacles, detouring round the tree was not feasible. In effect, if the baobab was not removed, the road could not be completed. It was a senseless situation.

Dirk Swannypoel, the team manager, had tried, but failed, to talk Chief Kinombwe into changing his mind.

'We should just go ahead and pull it down,' I said, but Dirk was reluctant, lest the action might appear provocative and enmesh us in precarious politics.

Neither of us believed that the baloney about ancestral phantoms was anything more than a red herring, but precisely what was behind the chief's obstinacy and perverted display of power, we were at a loss to understand. We were discussing that when a messenger arrived.

'Chief Kinombwe will speak with Tyrone Brown,' was the brief announcement.

'He's coming here?'

'He is waiting in the village. He is waiting for Tyrone Brown.'

'Why me?' I asked, though the answer was obvious.

I had little choice but to go along with this latest twist in his silly game, though I doubted the colour of my skin would make any difference to dead souls incarcerated* beneath a baobab tree.

* incarcerated: buried

As I glided the Range Rover over the smooth tarmac where, less than a year previously, there'd been only a rambling, token trail, I watched the silhouette of controversy loom ominously in the distance. Its grizzled fingers, protruding grotesquely from its obese trunk, seemed to mock me.

Stopping in front of it and removing my sunglasses to wipe away beads of sweat, I couldn't help wondering what kind of primitive reasoning I was up against. I looked once more at the gloomy relic and the two idle tractors, one on either side, with the heavy chains looped ready for the stumping, before bumping across the uneven ground towards the village of Kinombwe and the chief awaiting the arrival of the *mzungu** with the black skin.

While women and children congregated in doorways of wattle and daub dwellings, an elder stepped forward.

'Chief Kinombwe is waiting for you,' he said, and I was ushered towards and into a house slightly larger than the rest.

The chief, wearing a long *kitengi** cloth secured around his waist, sat on a stool in a corner. The thin light filtering in from outside cast distorting shadows, and even after I had removed my sunglasses and even after my eyes had adjusted to the dimness of the room, I could not see clearly the face which was assessing me. Even so, something in those concealed looks reminded me of someone.

The chief indicated a second stool and I sat awkwardly down.

'Welcome, Mr Brown,' he said, then, after a pause: 'Tell me, why is the road so important to you?'

---

* *mzungu*: white person
  kitengi: cotton cloth, usually brightly patterned

'The road is not for me. It is for you and your people.'

'We have lived long enough, well enough, without a road.'

'You will live better with one.'

'And why is that, Mr Brown?'

The contours of the chief's face moved rhythmically as he spoke, and once again I saw something familiar in the lines. This, though, was not the time to catalogue fleeting similarities.

'The road opens up immense possibilities, not only for agriculture but also for fishing.'

'Or perhaps other people might find it easier to come and steal our fish.'

Rational discussion was going to be difficult, but still I had to try.

'At the moment you grow only as much maize and relish as you yourselves can eat. Once the road is built, if your people can grow more, then they will be able to sell the extra in the towns, and with the money they get they will be able to buy salt, cooking oil, soap and all the other things they need.'

'And medicine and bicycles and education: all those things which you have in your country?'

'Yes,' I replied suspiciously.

I was still wondering about the direction of his reasoning when Chief Kinombwe spoke again.

'The road is good. We must indeed have the road.'

The man's unexpected positive statement puzzled me. Surely it wasn't going to be that easy? And it wasn't.

'The road is good,' repeated the chief. 'But the baobab is our problem. Do you understand why we Africans are afraid of pulling down such trees?'

'I've heard stories.'

'Only the weight of the mighty trunk holds down demonic forces. Destroy the tree and all manner of horrors could be unleashed.'

'I assure you, nothing will happen. No harm will come to your people.'

'You see us merely as superstitious villagers, don't you, Mr Brown?'

'No,' I lied, wondering what game the chief might now be planning. 'I respect your traditions, but if we are to build the road, the tree will have to go.'

'That in itself is a contradiction and tells me how little you understand us. I wonder how long you will stay in the country after the baobab has been removed; how long you will suffer the effects.'

'There won't be any effects.' I sounded very certain, but inside I was experiencing an unwelcome tinge of apprehension.

'Perhaps you should think about staying longer and getting to know us better. Then I too could learn about you and your country. We might even find that we are not so different after all, though our customs and traditions would have us believe otherwise.'

I was unimpressed with the suggestion, seeing it only as deliberate deviation away from the prime purpose of the meeting. But his voice, more than his words, bothered me. The fluency of his English had impressed, but now, was it my imagination or was his accent changing? Was he mimicking me?

'You speak excellent English,' I commented, curious.

'And why not? I was educated by excellent English people – at Mambalima Mission. Maybe you expected to find an ignorant illiterate, but in reality, lacking the material advantages of civilization does not make us backward. And we have other, less manifest advantages. We have history – personal history. We, the Lundas from the kingdom of Mwata Yamvo, have an identity. Tell me, Mr Brown, where do your ancestors come from?'

'My grandfather came from Trinidad.'

'And before that?'

My silence was the answer.

'You see – you, with all your trappings of civilization, have no identity, whereas we know every detail of our Lunda heritage.'

'When we first crossed the Luapula River, many hundreds of years ago, we found here the people of the Bwilile tribe. They had no chiefs, so we gave them chiefs and thus became the owners of the land. A chief is a very important person. He must always do the right thing, though that is not always easy. Take, for instance, the case of Sonjeli Kinombwe. He had two sons: twins. Who should be the next chief? How would you decide, Mr Brown?'

I ignored the question. I was not interested in history. I wanted to pull down the baobab so we could get on with building the road. But Kinombwe was not finished yet.

'Sonjeli discussed the problem at great lengths with the village elders. Finally it was decided that neither Nkuba nor Nachitu should become chief. Instead, the lineage should pass to the first son born to either of them. That child was Chiti, Nachitu's son. The ownership of the land would be vested in Chiti.

'Nkuba feigned happiness when his brother's son was born, but his heart was not in harmony with his smile. He wanted the land for his own son, as yet unborn. He waited many years, hoping that some natural disaster would overcome the child. When it did not, he took matters into his own hands. One blow across the head with a machete, and Chiti lay dead.

'Nkuba washed his hands in the river, but the blood of Chiti stayed with him. He could not escape from it. Wherever he went, he left behind a bloodied trail. Realizing he could not keep secret his foul deed, he fled. He hid in the swamps in the place which today we call *Chalalankuba* – "where Nkuba lay in hiding". But even there, Chiti's blood followed after him. The villagers, guided by the crimson trail, found him easily.

'Nkuba had committed treason. For that we have a punishment – we cut off an ear. After lopping off his ear, they banished him. What happened to Nkuba after that, we do not know. Maybe he fell prey to wild beasts, or maybe he was taken by the slave traders. Whatever, like your own forefathers, Nkuba lost his identity.

'Nachitu's wife gave birth to another son, the child who became Chief Makulu Kinombwe. And Chief Makulu had a son, who had a son, and so the line continued until you find me here today, descended from Nachitu and Makulu of the Kinombwes of the Lunda tribe.

'The spirit of Chiti rests beneath the baobab; that of his father Nachitu, too. And Nachitu remembers us from beneath the baobab. Do you know what I believe, Mr Brown? I believe that though the land is important, Nachitu thinks it is not worth the death of his son. I believe that Nachitu would release the land and the chieftainship to Nkuba and his descendants, in return for the life of his son, Chiti.

'But maybe I am wrong. Maybe instead Nachitu festers with ancient grievances. Should we risk unleashing those? Do we dare pull down the baobab?'

'I don't see we have a choice.'

'Oh, but we do. You can all go away now and leave the road where it is, or you can stay a while longer until it is completed. Do we pull down the tree?'

'Yes.'

'So be it. But we cannot ask others to perform the deed. You and I must bear the consequences of the act. The land is mine. The road is yours. The Baobab is ours. You and I should pull it down. Do you agree?' The chief stood up.

I stood up too. 'I agree.'

'I had to be sure you understood the implications. There are risks. We have no way of knowing what might happen.'

So reverently was the final warning given, that my mouth went dry and I began to question how far I might have misjudged the chief. What qualities had I, Tyrone Brown, with conceit constricting my vision, dismissed or refused to see?

For the first time I began to consider the possibility that uprooting the baobab might indeed involve something more than any normal stumping.

'Are you not afraid?' I asked.

'I am very afraid, Mr Brown; very afraid for both of us.'

My skin prickled, but I could not back down now. Instead, I thought about how it would feel to return to Dirk Swannypoel with a *fait accompli**.

We stepped, two erstwhile strangers, into the dazzle of the day. I raised my sunglasses protectively towards my eyes, but, before putting them on, turned to look at Chief Kinombwe, and saw him for the first time with unblemished vision. My own reflection smiled back at me. Shock precipitated panic, but I smothered my

---

* *fait accompli*: something which has already been done

response. Coincidence, I told myself – of a most raw kind, but coincidence nevertheless. That I had met a mirror image of myself must not affect the task we must perform. The baobab must still be stumped. Later, perhaps, we could remark on the quirk of destiny which had brought the road through the bush and ourselves to each other, but first to the tree, before either of us changed his mind.

I checked the chains around the tree, and their anchorage to the tractors, before we mounted.

There was a silence of expectancy in the surrounding bush as, revving the engines, we drove off along parallel paths, the heavy chains taut on the trunk behind us.

The tractors tugged; metal clanked. But the tree would not let go its hold on life. Then, propelled by an unknown element below the ground rather than by any force above, the roots were ripped asunder. With a roaring crash the tree was down. The devastating deed was done. A cloud of dust lingered in the air. The churned-up earth was pungent: old and rotten.

I waited for the floating debris to settle. It did not. Rather, its opacity intensified. Groping blindly I sought Kinombwe: called his name.

There were no reassuring words from him. There was only suffocating silence and a crushing sensation as fingers of forgotten ancestors clutched and clawed, and dragged me over the threshold and down into the vortex spun by other lives.

The spirit of my divided self struggling. My foetal soul passing through wombs, fusing in many versions, before entering the grim tenebrous[*] world held down for so long beneath the baobab.

---

[*]   tenebrous: dark

Acrid smells in dank mustiness. Mundane details obliterated as essentials coalesce in an otherwise encompassing darkness. A point of light. An image. A face. A man. Shrinking from myself, moving towards him and into him; my identity realized.

Holding the knife. Holding the child. Looking into his eyes: large eyes, pleading. Seeing his mouth open for the scream that cannot come, as the knife falls.

Smelling blood cavorting shamelessly: a cloying smell. Sweat permeating through the laden atmosphere. Those smells merging with others – the fetidness[*] of the swamps; decaying vegetation and the damp warmth of the sudd[*].

Voices slicing through the silence. Alien words becoming familiar; coming closer. Understanding those words. My own voice rising above the cacophony[*]; screams for mercy, scream of pain.

Blood again, this time my own. Voices drifting away.

Trudging through the void of the interior. Oppressive intensity of nothingness. Empty days and empty nights beneath a blighted sky.

New voices. New pain. Chafing irons smouldering around the ankles, wrists and neck. Red hot pain. Blood red sun. Outrage mellowing under the hostility of that.

Stale stench of sweat; rancid sour stink of fear. Most stringent smell of all: salt, not of tears nor sweat, but of water; stinging the skin, biting the lips.

Into the bowels of the boat with enormous flapping wings. Into darkness again.

Moving with the waves. More than an ear severed; a life too. Sailing away through the murky mists of time.

[*]   fetidness: foul smell   sudd: obtrusive floating vegetation
      cacophony: loud, discordant noise

Images fading, dissolving; out of reach. Sea breezes
blowing away the memories. A land breeze dispelling
the saltiness.

The poignant aroma of the earth seeped into my flesh,
caressed the wounds and touched my black man's soul.

I crawled out from the abyss and stepped away from
the bizarre meanderings of my mind, into burnishing
sunshine and a throbbing world. Birds warbled,
insects whirred and bullfrogs croaked. I breathed in
the sweetness of the land.

Kinombwe's stories had played strange tricks, but
now the giant tree was dead; the road could be
completed.

There Kinombwe; I told you so – no howling from
the dismal depths; no throwing up of ancient demons.
Those words I spoke in my mind, but in a tongue which
was not Tyrone Brown's. How could that be? Could
imagination be so strong; perception so acute?

But where was imagination to materialize the
wrenched-out tree with the gaping chasm? A road
concealed the facts; the road now cleaving its way
forwards into eternity.

The Kinombwe I'd known was gone. I stood there
alone, covered only by a mildewed cloth – the *kitengi*
he'd discarded.

As the slurred edges of reality sharpened, I looked
with ultimate clarity and I saw the child, and the cruel
scar crowning him. Reaching up, I felt the left side of
my face, where once I'd had an ear. The wound had
healed but, as with Chiti, the scar remained.

Chiti sits beside me now. Gone is he who wears the
clothes of Tyrone Brown and speaks his words. He has
my life. I have Nkuba's tainted legacy. I have the child

of the baobab. My identity, disseminated through the corridors of history, is whole again.

We've bathed in the time-spanning waters of the river and washed away the accumulation of the centuries. Now it is time to return to the village and the land for which Nkuba killed – the land which now is mine. Now I take Chiti home.

Footprints

Victor Kelleher

Benny hated his father's eager-beaver approach to weekends. His idea of the perfect Saturday was to get up late and spend the rest of the day doing nothing but recover from the week at school. Yet at his father's insistence here they were down near Sydney's Botanic Gardens in the early morning – and on one of his beloved Saturdays! – the pair of them jogging along the harbour foreshore through weather that had kept all but the most determined tourists indoors.

'Isn't this fun?' his father shouted above the roar of the wind.

And what a wind! It snatched at the overcast sky, sending unwary birds tumbling through the air like scraps of torn paper; it whipped the harbour into a frenzy, the grey waters erupting into ridges of fleeting white; it beat at the great Port Jackson fig trees until they creaked and groaned under the onslaught.

This is fun? Benny thought to himself, plodding wearily along. As far as he was concerned it was more like torture. Or worse, like being caught up in some ancient battle, with the whole of Sydney under siege from an unnamed force.

As though in opposition to that force, the wind shrieked louder than ever, bringing Benny to a stop. Even his father faltered. While over to their left there was a grinding, tearing sound followed by a frantic swish of limbs and leaves, and with a thump that made the whole slope tremble, one of the giant figs came crashing down.

'Come on,' his father insisted, straining forward, dismissing the fallen tree with a wave of the hand.

But Benny had had enough. 'Let's take a look,' he shouted back, and walked across to where the tree was lying forlornly on its side, its roots fanned out like the tentacles of some dead octopus.

He saw at once why it had fallen. The soil on this part of the slope was so thin that in spite of its buttressed root system the tree must always have been unstable. The only surprise was that it had not come down sooner. Where it had stood there was now an exposed shelf of sandstone, pinkish-grey and completely smooth except for two strangely familiar depressions in the surface. He peered closer. No, they were not really depressions, but marks *on* the surface, each a perfect mirror of the other. Like matching footprints. Or rather the smoky outline of someone's feet.

Benny recalled seeing similar outlines of hands during a trip to the Centre with his parents. Signatures, his father had called them, of Aborigines who had lived there long before. Well, were these a form of signature too? And if so, of whom? To judge from their size, whoever they had belonged to had not been particularly tall. Not much taller, perhaps, than Benny himself.

'We're wasting time,' his father shouted from the path, but Benny pretended he hadn't heard, even though the wind had swung round. Now it was pressing urgently from behind. And as if in obedience to its wishes, he let it push him forward, down into the shallow hole – let it guide him towards those two smoky outlines which were about the same size and shape as his own feet. They could almost have been his footprints, he considered idly, his signature, fretted there in another life and now awaiting his return.

A few last shuffling steps and his feet were covering them. *His* feet? So bare and brown? From the corner of his eye he glimpsed moving shadows, a mass of densely grown trees, an empty sky. He knew the sky could not really be empty. If he turned and looked, the tops of Sydney's skyscrapers would be clearly visible. He *did* turn, and all he could see, above a thick line of native bush, were racing clouds. Other darker forms were racing beneath the trees. Known voices were calling out to him. Repeating a name that was and was not his own.

'Bennelong! Bennelong!'

He stepped clear of the rock, his brown feet matching the hasty strides of those all about him. His body, surprisingly, as brown and bare as theirs.

An old woman, her breasts sagging, took his hand, and he slowed to a walk, letting the others run on ahead. Together, he and the woman climbed slowly down to the rocky shoreline: to where the seawall and the walkway had both magically disappeared, as though spirited away, the harbour water now lapping against stones and sand. The far shore had been equally transformed – reduced to an unbroken line of bush, with not a single house showing. He glanced behind him, confused, but the mown lawns and evenly spaced trees of the Botanic Gardens had also vanished, replaced by virgin forest. And the Bridge? The Opera House? Gone! The whole of the harbour was fringed with unblemished green, the grey of its waters interrupted only by a single canoe knifing in towards the shore, the paddles of the two fishermen gleaming in the pale light.

'The bad ones are coming, like before,' the old woman told him, and she tried to coax him back to the forest, treating him as a mother might treat a much-loved son.

But he resisted her, feeling oddly attracted by the excitement of the occasion. And by the whiff of danger too. It was not a new sensation. He seemed to remember having had a similar feeling as a small boy, not so many years earlier, when he or someone like him had sat before a glowing fire and listened to the story of how white ghosts had first visited this shore. They had come, the elders said, in an impossibly large boat. And before they left they had killed the warriors with sticks that spoke aloud.

'I have to see them,' he heard himself say, and reluctantly the old woman accompanied him. Clucking her disapproval as they moved round towards the outermost point of the bay, to where a crowd of people was already gathered. He, like everyone else, standing ankle-deep in shells, for this was a local midden, a place where countless generations of his people had feasted on shellfish from the harbour.

'They are not for us, these bad ones,' the woman murmured, in a voice that had surely spoken lovingly to him from his earliest years.

He nodded, pretending to agree with her, out of affection and respect; though secretly he was thrilled by the prospect of meeting these ghostly strangers. Fired by the thought that here and now the story of his childhood was about to take form.

'They're coming!'

The shout was taken up by those around him, and he pushed his way impatiently through the crowd, his bare feet crunching on the litter of shells.

'No!' the woman protested, clutching at his hand, but he dragged her with him to the water's edge.

Where at last he saw it. Bigger even than he had imagined and winged like a bird. The billows of its sails like clouds stolen from the sky spirits. The harbour waters parting obediently as it skimmed towards him.

People were beginning to edge nervously back along the point, making for the cover of the forest. But he could not tear himself from the spot, despite the woman's pleading. Fascinated, he watched the boat drift past; saw the white clouds of its sails close in upon themselves as it swung around and stopped. There were men climbing down its sides, just as they had in the story. Men in brightly coloured clothing, with long death-sticks in their hands. The same sticks which had once . . .

'Come! Come!' the woman begged him, breaking in upon his thoughts.

He turned towards her – her face, tear-stained and distressed, more familiar to him than any other, including his own which he had only ever glimpsed in the placid mirror of the waters. Her grief was also unnervingly familiar. Like a message to him from another time.

'You will die if you stay here,' she said tearfully.

And at once he knew that what she said was true. Knew it with a certainty she would never understand, for all her age and wisdom. He shivered as an invisible cloud, blown by unfelt winds, seemed to pass over the immensity of the land. A cloud that carried with it an ominous sense of tragedy.

Yet still the excitement and the longing remained alive within him. In the face of this known danger, he yearned still to greet these strange beings. To talk with them and share their minds, their ways. Turning his head, he cast a last passionate look across the bay, to where the mother of all boats was giving birth to smaller editions of itself: broad-beamed canoes in which men stood lined, the long sticks slung from their shoulders. He raised his hand in a half-hearted greeting and snatched it down again, dismayed by his own audacity. Then, in response to the woman's desperate pleas, he floundered with her across the heaped shells, the two of them heading for the trees as fast as her age and weariness would allow.

He could tell from her relieved expression that for her this was a welcome escape, a retreat to the safety of their old secure world. For him it was both more and less than that. A part of himself, he suspected, had been abandoned out there on the point. Marooned there. One day he might well return, in an attempt to make himself whole again. But not yet. Now was the time for flight.

A flight which, for that day at least, would have been complete had he not spied someone standing in the shadow of the trees, as though waiting for him. Not so much a person as the ghost of a person. Himself? Or one of those beings in the boat who had somehow reached this spot ahead of him?

He tried not to look more closely, fearful of what he might discover. But the temptation was too great. The sky over to his right suddenly crowded with a suggestion of towering shapes, the shimmering outline of giant trees reaching up around him.

Releasing the old woman's hand, he crept nearer, as drawn to this pale figure as he had been to the point beyond the bay or to the boat and the people in it. His bare feet shuffled forward, feeling their way across the platform of rock. The figure before him became even less definite – a vague silhouette that wavered and opened itself invitingly.

From somewhere in another life there came a wail of grief. The kind of keening cry reserved for the dead.

'Benne . . . !' the woman's voice sang out desperately.

The doleful sound was stolen by a sudden rise of wind and carried back to him in an altered form.

'Benny!'

A man's voice this time. A man's face peering into his.

'Benny? Are you all right?'

He changed his focus ever so slightly and saw again the Sydney he knew. With relief? He was not sure about that. The gentle parkland now appeared distinctly artificial; and there was something almost threatening about the high-rise buildings that loomed above the trees.

'I . . . I'm fine, Dad,' he said shakily, doing his best to sound unconcerned. 'Honest, I am.'

'You could have fooled me,' his father replied. 'You look as if you've seen a ghost.'

A ghost? He wondered whether that was all it had been. No. It had felt too real for that. As if in fact there were two Sydneys and he had somehow moved from one to the other and back again. As if there were two selves as well. He and that other person bound to each other by this place. This land – the real land, hidden beneath the mown lawns of the park.

Unnerved by his own thoughts, he stepped hastily clear of the footmarks on the rock.

'I felt a bit faint, that's all,' he muttered, giving a poor imitation of a smile.

'I shouldn't wonder,' his father responded. 'Anyone would feel faint if they lazed around as much as you do.

What you need is some decent exercise.' And to show what he meant he bounded off into the windswept day.

Benny followed less readily, jogging slowly across the lawns and down towards the water's edge. Although he had known that the sea wall would be there, he experienced a vague shock at actually encountering it. The sight of the Opera House and the Bridge also unsettled him slightly, as did the populated North Shore. Only the harbour itself seemed unaffected by the passage of time. On a day as boisterous as this, it was all but empty of craft. So much so that despite the rough weather Benny half expected to see a single canoe come arrowing in towards him. There was a flash of light on the water, and he stopped hopefully, but his father was calling out, banishing the illusion before it could take shape.

'Keep up!' he was yelling. 'Not far to go now.'

Benny ran on through the wind, past knots of Japanese and American tourists – many of them draped in cameras, others clinging to their hats – following the line of the bay just as those other bare brown feet had done all those years before. Round as far as the Opera House and then along the lower walkway to the furthermost point of land – a round-nosed promontory that thrust out into the harbour.

His father was waiting there for him, leaning against the rail and gazing out over the water. 'D'you know what they call this place?' he shouted, the wind whipping the words from his mouth as if intent on keeping them for itself.

Benny shook his head, though already he had half guessed the answer.

'Bennelong Point. Named after an Aboriginal who pined away out here. He was some kind of victim,

caught between two cultures, the black and the white.
Or so they reckon.'

Caught between two cultures . . .

The words seemed to touch something inside Benny
– something he had learned about long, long ago and
never really forgotten. The memory returning with
such force that again he felt a shock of surprised
recognition. Instinctively he spun around, searching
for a place he had lost and needed to find once more.

There was nothing there but the Opera House which
soared above him, and he stared up at it as though
seeing it for the first time. Never had those huge
curving shapes appeared less sail-like. Now they
reminded him of only one thing. Shells! Gigantic
versions of those same shells which had once crunched
beneath bare brown feet. Here! On this same spit of
land!

His father was bending over him inquiringly, a hand
on his shoulder. 'You feeling funny again, son?'

He shook himself free, impatiently, and swung back
towards the eastern end of the harbour. An
old-fashioned square-rigged ship was ploughing its
way up to the Point, as he had known it would be, with
just a rag of off-white sail fluttering from one of its
spars. No other ship in sight in all that grey expanse.
The dip of its bows so lifelike that for a few moments
he fully believed that he had taken another of those
invisible steps between worlds.

It was his father's voice that told him otherwise.
'Look over there. A replica of an old sailing vessel. Like
something from the days of early settlement. Built for
the tourist trade most probably. I'm surprised it's out
in weather like this.'

Benny was not surprised, however. Not any longer.

'It looks real enough to me,' he said sadly, speaking half to himself, half to the wind which drove in hard across the Point, the wail of its passage mimicking the cry of a long unanswered voice.

'What did you say?' his father asked, cupping a hand to his ear.

But Benny could not have explained even if he had wanted to. Except perhaps to Bennelong.

──────────── Money Matters ────────────

Shiva Naipaul *was born in 1945 in Port of Spain, Trinidad. When he died in 1985, aged forty, David Holloway wrote in* The Daily Telegraph: *'We have lost one of the most talented and wide-ranging writers of his generation.' During his life, Shiva Naipaul's novels and short stories won many awards.*

The stories of **R.K. Narayan**, *including* Cat Within *are set in the imaginary village of Malgudi in India. The residents of Malgudi come from all walks of life. There are wealthy people and poor people, young and old, saints and sinners, those who achieve success and those who fail.*

In Shiva Naipaul's story, Mr Sookhoo gets his just deserts when his fraudulent money-making scheme is exposed. Similarly, in Cat Within, *a property owner who has been less than consider-ate to his tenants is shown up for what he is when a cat jumps into a brass jug, and the exorcist is called.*

Mr Sookhoo and the Carol Singers
Shiva Naipaul

Mr Sookhoo, a short, fat man with a pot belly and a bushy, black moustache, drove the only truck in the village. He carried anything people would pay him to carry: furniture, sand, gravel; and, when the village headmaster asked, he took the schoolchildren on excursions to the beach, sugar-cane factories and oil refineries. It was a way of life that Mr Sookhoo found entirely to his liking: he was his own boss.

He was rocking slowly on his veranda, scraping thoughtfully at his teeth with a toothpick, when his wife appeared through the doorway.

'Eh, man. For the past two days all you doing is sitting here and rocking. Mr Ali tired ask you to carry

47

that gravel to Port of Spain for him. What's more, he pay you for it already.'

'Ali could wait.' Mr Sookhoo continued to pick his teeth. 'So you been wondering what I been doing these past two days, eh?' He tossed the toothpick over the veranda rail and Mrs Sookhoo followed its flight with interest. 'All you could see was me rocking. But there was something else I was doing. Something invisible.' He smiled slyly at her. 'I was *thinking*.'

'Thinking!' Mrs Sookhoo weighed the significance of this remark. It worried her. 'Be careful, man. I sure it not good for you.'

Mr Sookhoo laughed scornfully. 'Now and then a man have to do a bit of thinking. Otherwise . . .' Losing the thread of his argument, he shrugged.

'I still think you should deliver that gravel to Mr Ali.'

'Ali could go to hell.' Mr Sookhoo expanded his chest.

'But what get into you so all of a sudden, man? I know all this thinking wasn't good for you.'

Mr Sookhoo waved a finger at her. 'I just been working out a master plan. Tell me – how many days it have till Christmas?'

Mrs Sookhoo frowned. 'The radio say it have about twenty-seven or so shopping days to go.'

'Right!' Mr Sookhoo gazed fiercely at her. 'Christmas is coming and the geese is getting fat. Time to put a penny in the old man hat.' He took another toothpick from his pocket. 'Believe me when I tell you the geese is really going to be fat this year. And it going to have so many pennies in the old man hat by Boxing Day that you will bawl when you see them.'

Mrs Sookhoo could not disguise her alarm. 'What get into you so sudden, man?'

'Tell me,' he went on, scraping vigorously at his teeth, 'tell me how much children it have in the school?'

'Twenty, thirty . . .'

'To be on the safe side, let me say it have twenty-five. Twenty-five divide by five is five. Agree?' Mr Sookhoo tossed the toothpick over the veranda rail and, as before, his wife followed its flight with interest. He got up from the rocking-chair and leaned against the rail, staring up at the sky. 'So that if I divide them up into five groups and say each time they sing they get a little dollar or so . . .'

'What you intending to do, man? You sure is legal?'

He ignored her. '. . . and say each group sing about ten time a night for twenty or so nights . . .' Here the magnitude of his calculations so affected Mr Sookhoo that he let out a prolonged whistle, slapped his stomach and spat on a rose-bush. 'Of course I'll have to take the cost of the gasoline into account.' A shadow crossed his face. 'Still . . .'

'You going to land in jail, Sookhoo.'

'Chut, woman! People like hearing little children sing. Once you could organize it properly, it have a lot of money in it. All this carol singing need is organization.'

'You forgetting one thing.'

'What?' Mr Sookhoo asked sharply.

'You is a Hindu.'

He laughed. 'Who is to know that in Port of Spain? It have hundreds of Christians out there who look just like me. Like you never hear of the Reverend Hari Lal Singh?'

'I still don't like it. And another thing. All them children you does see singing carol singing for charity.'

'That is what they would like people like you and me to believe. All that money they does collect going straight into their own pocket. Charity!' Mr Sookhoo spat disdainfully on the rose-bush and went inside.

Mr Sookhoo changed into his best suit and left the house pursued by his wife's anxious enquiries. He walked the half-mile to the village school with a quick, firm step.

Mr Archibald, the headmaster, stared at him suspiciously from behind the pile of copybooks he was correcting. He was well aware that Mr Sookhoo grossly overcharged him for the school's excursions.

'Good afternoon, Head. How is life with you these days?' Mr Sookhoo hummed under his breath.

'As usual.' Mr Archibald was guarded. 'I think I know that tune you're humming', he said. 'Christmas is coming and the geese are getting fat. Time to . . .'

'First time I hear of that one, Head. You wouldn't imagine how sometimes I does regret not having a education. It must be a great thing.'

Mr Archibald looked doubtfully at him. 'I suppose you have a reason for coming to see me, Mr Sookhoo?'

Mr Sookhoo leaned his elbows confidentially on the desk. 'I'll come straight to the point, Head. They asking me to organize a charity.'

Mr Archibald dried his forehead with a handkerchief, a symptom of his incredulity. 'They asking *you* to organize a charity, Mr Sookhoo? Who asking you to organize a charity?'

'The Deaf, Dumb and Blind Institute. They want me to help organize a little carol singing for them.'

'I never knew such an Institute existed.'

'Is a new thing.'

'Ah. But why *you*, Mr Sookhoo? Not that I want to be rude, but to be frank . . .'

Mr Sookhoo smiled gallantly. 'I not offended, Head. I know that my life – up until now that is – hasn't been exactly perfect. Like most men I have a few faults . . .'

'A few!'

Mr Sookhoo laughed. 'I don't know how to say this, Head – it going to sound funny coming from a man like me – but, all the same, I think I finally see the light.'

'What light?'

'Head! How you mean "what light"? That don't sound nice coming from a man like you, a man of education.'

Mr Archibald's vanity was touched. 'Sorry, Mr Sookhoo. But, as you yourself said, coming from a man like you . . .'

'Sooner or later a man have to set his mind on higher things,' Mr Sookhoo intervened solemnly.

'That is something nobody can teach us, Mr Sookhoo.' Mr Archibald's eyes swept vaguely across the ceiling. Then they hardened, assuming a more businesslike expression. 'But why *you*, Mr Sookhoo? That is what I still don't understand. Even accepting that you have seen the . . . the light, it's very odd that the Deaf, Dumb and Blind Institute should ask you to . . .'

'Transport, Head. Transport.' And he added hastily: 'Don't think I is the only one. I only in charge of one area, you understand. This is a big operation they have plan.'

Mr Archibald nodded. 'Where do I come into it?'

Mr Sookhoo leaned closer to him. 'Not you so much as your pupils. This is a chance for them to help out a worthy cause by singing a few carols. My truck is at their disposal. Don't worry – is I who going to be paying for the gasoline.'

Mr Archibald stared at him. 'I really don't know what to say, Mr Sookhoo. Your generosity is overwhelming.' He fluttered the handkerchief before his face.

Mr Sookhoo grinned broadly. 'You teach them to sing a few carol and I take them to Port of Spain in the truck free of charge. That's a deal.' He held out his hand.

'Your generosity is overwhelming, Mr Sookhoo.'

'Is because I see the light,' Mr Sookhoo said.

It took Mr Archibald a week to teach his pupils a repertoire of six carols. Mr Sookhoo went to the school every afternoon to listen to them practise. Standing at the back of the classroom, he would shout encouragingly at them. 'That's the way, kiddies. Remember it's a worthy cause you singing for.'

Mr Archibald, beaming, would swing his baton (in fact a whip) with renewed vigour.

The first expedition into Port of Spain was a gay affair. Mr Sookhoo polished his truck and drove to the school. Freshly washed and dressed in white, the children looked convincing. Mr Archibald provided them with candles. 'I felt it was the least I could do considering you giving the gasoline,' he explained to Mr Sookhoo. They drove to one of the richer suburbs of the city and Mr Sookhoo parked his truck discreetly in a narrow side-street. He gathered the children about him, dividing them into groups of five.

'It have two things I must tell you about,' he said when he had finished. 'First and most important – don't mention my name to nobody . . .'

'Why?'

Mr Sookhoo glowered at the questioner, a small, earnest boy.

'Because I is a modest kind of person, that's why. If they ask who send you say is the Deaf, Dumb and Blind Institute. And if they say they never hear of that before, tell them is a new thing just open up. You understand?' The children nodded confusedly. 'Second. Try to get a dollar each time you sing. When they pay you, stop. What would be the point in singing more after that, eh?' Mr Sookhoo giggled. The earnest boy gazed sternly at him. Mr Sookhoo, catching his eye, turned away in discomfort. The groups dispersed and, fetching a deep sigh, he took a toothpick from his pocket and scratched contentedly at his front teeth.

The choirs met with immoderate success. Their renditions were listened to attentively and no one gave them less than a dollar. In all, Mr Sookhoo collected just over forty dollars. He was jubilant.

'Good work.'

'Mr Sookhoo . . .' the earnest boy began.

'Later, sonny, later.'

'Have a look at that, woman.' Mr Sookhoo displayed the night's takings to his wife. 'Forty dollars in hard cash. And how? By using the brains God give me. By thinking. That's how.'

'Some people does call it embezzling. They bound to find out sooner or later what you doing.'

'How they go find out?' Mr Sookhoo folded the notes and put them in his pocket.

Success stimulated ambition. 'We going to start earlier and finish later,' he informed the children the next day. The choirs were not quite as gay as they had been the night before, but they set about their task without complaint. That night Mr Sookhoo collected fifty-five dollars. He could hardly contain himself, counting the notes again and again. 'Organization was all it needed,' he said to himself.

'Mr Sookhoo . . .'

'Later, sonny, later.'

Mr Sookhoo prospered for a whole week. He had collected over three hundred dollars. And there were still many shopping days to Christmas. And there were still several suburbs waiting to be plundered. His eyes glittered. 'You going to end up in jail, Sookhoo,' his wife warned. He laughed and continued his calculations.

Early one morning Mr Archibald came to see him.

'How things going, Mr Sookhoo?'

'As well as could be expected in the circumstances, Head.'

'You not collecting enough?'

'Is a hard business, Head. These rich people tight, tight with they money.'

Mr Archibald dried his forehead with a handkerchief. 'You know Horace?'

'Which one is Horace?' Mr Sookhoo's heart sank.

'A thin little boy. He say that you working them down to the ground and that you collecting one hell of a lot of money.'

'I always thought he was a trouble-maker.'

'That boy is my brightest pupil, Mr Sookhoo. He's going to go far.'

'They is the worst kind.' Mr Sookhoo spat on the rose-bush.

Mr Archibald cleared his throat. 'You sure you being honest and above board with me, Mr Sookhoo? I mean this Institute really exist, not so?'

Mr Sookhoo gave the headmaster a pained look. 'Head! Head! How you could say a thing like that to me? A man of your education to boot!'

'Just put my mind at rest, Mr Sookhoo. You really see the light?' Mr Archibald spoke in a whisper.

Mr Sookhoo rested a comforting hand on the headmaster's shoulder. 'Honest to God, Head. I really see the light.'

Mr Archibald relaxed. He was anxious to believe Mr Sookhoo.

'These children working real hard,' he said. 'You could buy them a little sweet drink and ice-cream every day. I'm sure the Institute wouldn't mind.'

'Anything you say, Head. But I'll have to tell the Institute about it.'

'I could do that for you. I don't want them to think you're cheating them.'

'Don't bother yourself, Head. They trust me.'

Mr Archibald smiled and left the house.

The following night – it was the second week of their carolling – Mr Sookhoo took the children to the Trinidad Dairies. He bought them a Coca-cola each. When they had finished Mr Sookhoo got up to go.

'You forgetting something,' Horace said.

Mr Sookhoo instinctively felt for his wallet. His hand caressed the square lump. 'What it is I forgetting, Mr Know-All?'

The children gathered in an expectant circle.

'Mr Archibald tell you to buy ice-cream for we.'

Mr Sookhoo scowled. 'They don't sell ice-cream here.'

Horace appealed to the other children for support.

'I just see somebody buy a ice-cream,' one of them said.

'Well, I say they don't sell ice-cream here. And therefore they don't. You understand?'

'I know for a fact they does sell ice-cream here,' Horace insisted. 'To tell you the truth, I believe you trying to cheat we, Mr Sookhoo. I believe you keeping all that money we been getting for yourself.' Horace pouted insolently.

For a moment Mr Sookhoo hesitated, resisting the temptation to slap Horace. Finally he said: 'You little sonofabitch!'

'All you hear what he call me? You hear? Looking greatly aggrieved, Horace walked away from the bar.

'I feel like letting that sonofabitch find his own way home.' Unhappily, he could read no sympathy on the faces of the choir.

Mr Archibald had a visitor.

'I come to ask a favour of you, Headmaster.'

'I will do anything in my power to help you, sir,' Mr Archibald replied primly.

'I'm involved in charity work . . .'

'I myself have been having a little experience of that.'

'Have you? Well, I was wondering if your pupils would care to sing carols for my charity. We choose certain schools each year . . .'

Mr Archibald smiled sympathetically. 'I'm afraid we're already booked up this year. I'm sorry.'

'I understand. As I always say at times like these, one charity is as good as another. The unfortunate, no matter what their affliction, are always to be succoured.'

For some seconds both men savoured their goodness.

'Incidentally, Headmaster – and I hope you don't mind my asking you . . .'

'Not at all, sir. I have no secrets.'

'What charity are your pupils singing for?'

'The Deaf, Dumb and Blind Institute. I believe it's a new thing just opened up a few months ago.'

His visitor started. There was a long silence while they looked at each other.

'That's very strange, Headmaster. You see, I work for something called the Blind Institute. But the Deaf, Dumb *and* Blind Institute . . . luckily I have a list of accredited charities here with me.' He took a pamphlet from his pocket and scanned it.

'I feel quite faint.' Mr Archibald fluttered his handkerchief.

'Pardon me for saying so, Headmaster, but I think you've been taken for a ride.'

'I really do feel quite faint.'

Trinidad is a small island in a small world.

When Mr Ali saw the group of children led by Horace coming confidently up the path towards him and singing 'Silent Night', he lost his temper.

'Stop that blasted racket this minute!'

The choir stuttered into silence, their candles guttering in the wind. Loose gravel shifted under their feet. It had been their rudest welcome to date.

'Tell me who it is send you to disturb my peace.'

'Is the Deaf, Dumb and Blind Institute what send we.'

'The Deaf, Dumb and Blind Institute, eh! Try me with another one.'

'Is a new thing. Just open up these last few months,' one of the children ventured timidly. He looked round for Horace, their acknowledged leader. But Horace had detached himself from the group and stood to one side, lost in contemplation.

'You have any identification?' Mr Ali was very threatening.

The child cringed. 'Ask Horace over there. He will know.'

Mr Ali strode over to Horace. 'Tell me who send you,' he shouted. 'And remember no lies, if you not careful I'll skin the whole lot of you alive.'

Horace smirked. 'Is Mr Sookhoo who send we.'

'Mr Sookhoo! He have a moustache and big belly?'

Horace nodded.

'And he does drive a truck?'

'He park just down the road waiting for we to come back.'

'And what about this so-called Institute? It have any truth in that?'

'Mr Sookhoo make that up.' Horace's smirk intensified.

'What a tricky bugger, eh! So that's why he wasn't delivering my gravel. Come and show me where Mr Sookhoo is, Horace. I have a little outstanding business to settle with him.'

Horace, abandoning his candle, skipped eagerly down the path, followed by Mr Ali and the nonplussed[*] choir.

Mr Sookhoo was sitting in his truck, sucking a toothpick and occasionally looking at his watch. A notebook lay open on his lap covered with scrawled calculations. The confused sound of children's voices reached him. 'How come they so early tonight?' he wondered, peering into the rear-view mirror. He stiffened. The toothpick hung limp between his teeth.

'Mr Sookhoo! I so glad I manage to catch up with you at last. I been longing to have a chat with you.' Mr Ali's voice floated sweetly on the night air.

'Believe me when I say you still have a lot of catching up to do,' Mr Sookhoo muttered. He flung the

*   nonplussed: bewildered, puzzled

toothpick out of the window. The engine stammered into life and the truck lurched away from the curb, gathering speed.

'Don't think you getting away this time, Mr Sookhoo.'

'Mr Sookhoo! Mr Sookhoo! Wait for we! Wait for we!'

The cries of the choir faded behind him, drowned by the noise of the engine.

'Woman, bring your clothes quick! I think we have to go away from here for a while. Things hotting up.' Mr Sookhoo raced up the steps to the veranda and stood there catching his breath.

'Good evening, Mr Sookhoo.' Two large policemen came strolling casually through the sitting-room door, flourishing torches.

Mr Sookhoo clutched at his heart. However, he recovered himself quickly. 'Why is you, sergeant.'

Mr Archibald trailed behind them, accompanied by his visitor. Mrs Sookhoo, her cheeks wet with tears, brought up the rear.

'Man . . . man,' she moaned.

Mr Sookhoo paid her no attention. 'Why, Head – you here too. And I see you bring a friend with you as well.'

'You deceived me, Mr Sookhoo. A most cruel deception.'

Mr Sookhoo gestured resignedly.

'I really thought you had seen the light, Mr Sookhoo.' Mr Archibald seemed on the verge of tears.

The sergeant produced a notebook and licked the tip of his pencil. 'Mr Sookhoo will see a lot of lights in jail,' he said quietly and started to write.

Mrs Sookhoo moaned louder.

'This gentleman,' the sergeant went on, indicating Mr Archibald's visitor, 'is from the Blind Institute. Show him your card, Mr Harris.'

Mr Harris showed Mr Sookhoo his card.

He refused to look at it. 'I know all them tricks,' Mr Sookhoo said. 'Ask him how much money he does make out of it. Go on. Ask him.'

Mr Harris flushed. 'I get paid a salary for the work I do, Mr Sookhoo. Legally. Just because I work for charity doesn't mean I can live on air.'

'Living on air my arse! You see the expensive clothes he wearing? I could tell you where he get the money to buy all that.'

'This is to add insult to injury,' Mr Harris said.

'I should warn you, Mr Sookhoo, that everything you say will be taken down in evidence against you.' The sergeant scribbled energetically.

A sleek motor-car stopped outside the gate. Horace and Mr Ali entered out of breath.

'Ali! Like is a party we having here tonight.'

'I'm not in a party mood, Mr Sookhoo. I come for all that money I pay you to deliver my gravel.'

'What gravel is this?' the sergeant asked interestedly.

Mr Ali outlined his grievances.

'The plot thickens,' the sergeant said.

'Man, remember how I did tell you all this thinking would be bad for you. Remember . . .'

'Go and do something useful, woman. Bring me a toothpick.'

Horace sidled up to Mr Archibald. He tugged at his trousers. 'He didn't buy we any ice-cream either. And you should have hear how he insult me when I remind him.'

'Don't worry, Horace. Mr Sookhoo is going to get what he deserves.' Mr Archibald patted Horace.

'I think you should expel that boy from your school, Head. He's a born sonofabitch.' Mr Sookhoo spat on the rose-bush.

'You hear the kind of thing he does call me?' Horace exclaimed aggrievedly.

The sergeant closed his notebook. 'You better come to the station with us, Mr Sookhoo. You could make your statement there – for what it's worth.'

Sandwiched between the two policemen, Mr Sookhoo was escorted to the waiting car. He waved to the small crowd that had assembled on the pavement.

'Don't say I never warn you, Sookhoo.'

Mr Sookhoo smiled at his wife. 'You didn't bring me that toothpick.' He laughed.

The car drove off.

'The Good Lord is just. Isn't he, Horace?' Mr Archibald curled an affectionate arm around the boy.

'Yes.' Horace grinned and thought with delight of the ice-cream Mr Archibald had promised to buy him.

Cat Within

R. K. Narayan

A passage led to the back yard, where a well and a lavatory under a large tamarind tree served the needs of the motley tenants of the ancient house in Vinayak Mudali Street; the owner of the property, by partitioning and fragmenting all the available space, had managed to create an illusion of shelter and privacy for his hapless tenants and squeezed the maximum rent out of everyone, himself occupying a narrow ledge abutting the street, where he had a shop selling, among other things, sweets, pencils and ribbons to children swarming from the municipal school across the street. When he locked up for the night, he slept across the doorway so that no intruder should pass without first stumbling on him; he also piled up cunningly four empty kerosene tins inside the dark shop so that at the slightest contact they should topple down with a clatter: for him a satisfactory burglar alarm.

Once at midnight a cat stalking a mouse amidst the grain bags in the shop noticed a brass jug in its way and thrust its head in out of curiosity. The mouth of the jug was not narrow enough to choke the cat or wide enough to allow it to withdraw its head. Suddenly feeling the weight of a crown and a blinker over its eyes at the same time, the cat was at first puzzled and then became desperate. It began to jump and run around, hitting its head with a clang on every wall. The shopkeeper, who had been asleep at his usual place, was awakened by the noise in the shop. He peered through a chink into the dark interior, quickly withdrew his head and cried into the night, 'Thief! Thief! Help!' He also seized a bamboo staff and started tapping it challengingly on the ground. Every time the staff came down, the jar-crowned cat jumped high and about and banged its hooded head against every possible object, losing its sanity completely. The shopman's cry woke up his tenants and brought them crowding around him. They peered through the chink in the door and shuddered whenever they heard the metallic noise inside. They looked in again and again, trying vainly to make out in the darkness the shape of the phantom, and came to the conclusion, 'Oh, some devilish creature, impossible to describe it.' Someone ventured to suggest, 'Wake up the exorcist.' Among the motley crowd boxed in that tenement was also a professional exorcist. Now he was fast asleep, his living portion being at the farthest end.

He earned fifty rupees a day without leaving his cubicle; a circle of clients always waited at his door. His clients were said to come from even distant Pondicherry and Ceylon and Singapore. Some days they would be all over the place, and in order not to frighten the other tenants, he was asked to meet his clients in the back yard, where you would find assembled any day a dozen hysterical women and demented men, with their relatives holding them down. The exorcist never emerged from his habitation without the appropriate makeup for his role – his hair matted and coiled up high, his untrimmed beard combed down to flutter in the wind, his forehead splashed with sacred ash, vermilion* and

* vermilion: scarlet dye

sandal paste*, and a rosary of rare, plum-sized beads from the Himalayan slopes around his throat. He possessed an ancient palm-leaf book in which everyone's life was supposed to be etched in mysterious couplets. After due ceremonials, he would sit on the ground in front of the clients with the book and open a particular page appropriate to each particular individual and read out in a singsong manner. No one except the exorcist could make out the meaning of the verse composed in antiquated Tamil* of a thousand years ago. Presently he would explain: 'In your last life you did certain acts which are recoiling on you now. How could it be otherwise? It is karma*. This seizure will leave you on the twenty-seventh day and tenth hour after the next full moon, this karma will end . . . Were you at any time . . .?' He elicited much information from the parties themselves. 'Was there an old woman in your life who was not well-disposed to you? Be frank.' 'True, true,' some would say after thinking over it, and they would discuss it among themselves and say, 'Yes, yes, must be that woman Kamu . . .' The exorcist would then prescribe the course of action: 'She has cast a spell. Dig under the big tree in your village and bring any bone you may find there, and I'll throw it into the river. Then you will be safe for a while.' Then he would thrash the victim with a margosa* twig, crying, 'Be gone at once, you evil spirit.'

---

* sandal paste: a paste made from fragrant wood
  Tamil: a language of south-east India
  karma: the result of the actions of a person's life
  margosa: an oil- bearing Indian tree

On this night the shopman in his desperation pushed his door, calling, 'Come out, I want your help . . . Strange things are going on; come on.'

The exorcist hurriedly slipped on his rosary and, picking up his bag, came out. Arriving at the trouble-spot he asked, 'Now, tell me what is happening!'

'A jug seems to have come to life and bobs up and down, hitting everything around it bang-bang.'

'Oh, it's the jug-spirit, is it! It always enters and animates an empty jug. That's why our ancients have decreed that no empty vessel should be kept with its mouth open to the sky but always only upside down. These spirits try to panic you with frightening sounds. If you are afraid, it might hit your skull. But I can deal with it.'

The shopman wailed, 'I have lived a clean and honest life, never harmed a soul, why should this happen to me?'

'Very common, don't worry about it. It's karma, your past life . . . In your past life you must have done something.'

'What sort of thing?' asked the shopman with concern.

The exorcist was not prepared to elaborate his thesis[*]. He hated his landlord as all the other tenants did, but needed more time to frame a charge and go into details. Now he said gently, 'This is just a mischievous spirit, nothing more, but weak-minded persons are prone to get scared and may even vomit blood.' All this conversation was carried on to the accompaniment of the clanging metal inside the shop. Someone in the crowd cried, 'This is why you must

[*] elaborate his thesis: expand on his explanation

have electricity. Every corner of this town has electric lights. We alone have to suffer in darkness.'

'Why don't you bring in a lantern?'

'No kerosene for three days, and we have been eating by starlight.'

'Be patient, be patient,' said the house-owner, 'I have applied for power. We will get it soon.'

'If we had electric lights we could at least have switched them on and seen that creature, at least to know what it is.'

'All in good time, all in good time, sir, this is no occasion for complaints.' He led the exorcist to the shop entrance. Someone flourished a flashlight, but its battery was weak and the bulb glowed like embers, revealing nothing. Meanwhile, the cat, sensing the presence of a crowd, paused, but soon revived its activity with redoubled vigour and went bouncing against every wall and window bar. Every time the clanging sound came the shopman trembled and let out a wail, and the onlookers jumped back nervously. The exorcist was also visibly shaken. He peered into the dark shop at the door and sprang back adroitly every time the metallic noise approached. He whispered, 'At least light a candle; what a man to have provided such darkness for yourself and your tenants, while the whole city is blazing with lights. What sort of a man are you!'

Someone in the crowd added, 'Only a single well for twenty families, a single lavatory!'

A wag added, 'When I lie in bed with my wife, the littlest whisper between us is heard on all sides.'

Another retorted, 'But you are not married.'

'What if? There are others with families.'

'None of your business to become a champion for others. They can look after themselves.'

Bang! Bang!

'It's his sinfulness that has brought this haunting,' someone said, pointing at the shopman.

'Why don't you all clear out if you are so unhappy?' said the shopman. There could be no answer to that, as the town like all towns in the world suffered from a shortage of housing. The exorcist now assumed command. He gestured to others to keep quiet. 'This is no time for complaints or demands. You must all go back to bed. This evil spirit inside has to be driven out. When it emerges there must be no one in its way, otherwise it'll get under your skin.'

'Never mind, it won't be worse than our landlord. I'd love to take the devil under my skin if I can kick these walls and bring down this miserable ramshackle on the head of whoever owns it,' said the wag. The exorcist said, 'No, no, no harsh words, please . . . I'm also a tenant and suffer like others, but I won't make my demands now. All in proper time. Get me a candle –' He turned to the shopman. 'Don't you sell candles? What sort of a shopman are you without candles in your shop!' No one lost his chance to crucify the shopman.

He said, 'Candles are in a box on the right-hand side on a shelf as you step in – you can reach it if you just stretch your arm . . . '

'You want me to go in and try? All right, but I charge a fee for approaching a spirit – otherwise I always work from a distance.' The shopman agreed to the special fee and the exorcist cleared his throat, adjusted his coiffure* and stood before the door of the shop proclaiming loudly, 'Hey, spirit, I'm not afraid, I know your kind too well, you know me well,

---

* coiffure: hairdo

so . . . ' He slid open the shutter, stepped in gingerly; when he had advanced a few steps, the jug hit the ventilator glass and shattered it, which aggravated the cat's panic, and it somersaulted in confusion and caused a variety of metallic pandemonium in the dark chamber; the exorcist's legs faltered, and he did not know for a moment what his next step should be or what he had come in for. In this state he bumped into the piled-up kerosene tins and sent them clattering down, which further aggravated the cat's hysteria. The exorcist rushed out unceremoniously. 'Oh, oh, this is no ordinary affair. It seizes me like a tornado . . . it'll tear down the walls soon.'

'*Aiyo**!' wailed the shopman.

'I have to have special protection . . . I can't go in . . . no candle, no light. We'll have to manage in the dark. If I hadn't been quick enough, you would not have seen me again.'

'*Aiyo*! What's to happen to my shop and property?'

'We'll see, we'll see, we will do something,' assured the other heroically; he himself looking eerie in the beam of light that fell on him from the street. The shopman was afraid to look at him, with his grisly face and rolling eyes, whose corners were touched with white sacred ash. He felt he had been caught between two devils – difficult to decide which one was going to prove more terrible, the one in the shop or the one outside. The exorcist sat upright in front of the closed door as if to emphasize, 'I'm not afraid to sit here,' and commanded, 'Get me a copper pot, a copper tumbler and a copper spoon. It's important.'

'Why copper?'

---

* *Aiyo*!: Have mercy!

'Don't ask questions . . . All right, I'll tell you: because copper is a good conductor. Have you noticed electric wires of copper overhead?'

'What is it going to conduct now?'

'Don't ask questions. All right, I'll tell you. I want a medium which will lead my mantras* to that horrible thing inside.'

Without further questioning, the shopman produced an aluminum pot from somewhere. 'I don't have copper, but only aluminum . . . '

'In our country let him be the poorest man, but he'll own a copper pot . . . But here you are calling yourself a *sowcar*, you keep nothing; no candle, no light, no copper . . . ' said the exorcist.

'In my village home we have all the copper and silver . . . '

'How does it help you now? It's not your village house that is now being haunted, though I won't guarantee this may not pass on there . . . Anyway, let me try.' He raised the aluminum pot and hit the ground; immediately from inside came the sound of the jug hitting something again and again. 'Don't break the vessel,' cried the shopman. Ignoring his appeal the exorcist hit the ground again and again with the pot. 'That's a good sign. Now the spirits will speak. We have our own code.' He tapped the aluminum pot with his knuckles in a sort of Morse code. He said to the landlord, 'Don't breathe hard or speak loudly. I'm getting a message: I'm asked to say it's the spirit of someone who is seeking redress. Did you wrong anyone in your life?'

'Oh, no, no,' said the shopman in panic. 'No, I've always been charitable . . . '

---

* mantras: incantations

The exorcist cut him short. 'Don't tell me anything, but talk to yourself and to that spirit inside. Did you at any time handle . . . wait a minute, I'm getting the message . . . ' He held the pot's mouth to his ear. 'Did you at any time handle someone else's wife or money?'

The shopman looked horrified. 'Oh, no, never.'

'Then what is it I hear about you holding a trust for a widow . . . ?'

He brooded while the cat inside was hitting the ventilator, trying to get out. The man was in a panic now. 'What trust? May I perish if I have done anything of that kind. God has given me enough to live on . . . '

'I've told you not to talk unnecessarily. Did you ever molest any helpless woman or keep her at your mercy? If you have done a wrong in your childhood, you could expiate . . . '

'How?'

'That I'll explain, but first confess . . . '

'Why?'

'A true repentance on your part will emasculate the evil spirit.' The jug was hitting again, and the shopman became very nervous and said, 'Please stop that somehow, I can't bear it.' The exorcist lit a piece of camphor, his stock-in-trade, and circled the flame in all directions. 'To propitiate* the benign* spirits around so that they may come to our aid . . .' The shopman was equally scared of the benign spirits. He wished, at that pale starlit hour, that there were no spirits whatever, good or bad. Sitting on the pyol, and hearing the faint shrieking of a night bird flying across

---

*   propitiate: to appease, to win goodwill
    benign: good, kind

the sky and fading, he felt he had parted from the solid world of men and material and had drifted on to a world of unseen demons.

The exorcist now said, 'Your conscience should be clear like the Manasaro Lake. So repeat after me whatever I say. If there is any cheating, your skull will burst. The spirit will not hesitate to dash your brains out.'

'Alas, alas, what shall I do?'

'Repeat after me these words: I have lived a good and honest life.' The shopman had no difficulty in repeating it, in a sort of low murmur in order that it might not be overheard by his tenants. The exorcist said, 'I have never cheated anyone.'

' . . . cheated anyone,' repeated the shopman.

'Never appropriated anyone's property . . . '

The shopman began to repeat, but suddenly stopped short to ask, 'Which property do you mean?'

'I don't know,' said the exorcist, applying the pot to his ear. 'I hear of some irregularity.'

'Oh, it's not my mistake . . . ' the shopman wailed. 'It was not my mistake. The property came into my hands, that's all . . . '

'Whom did it belong to?'

'Honappa, my friend and neighbour, I was close to his family. We cultivated adjoining fields. He wrote a will and was never seen again in the village.'

'In your favour?'

'I didn't ask for it; but he liked me . . . '

'Was the body found?'

'How should I know?'

'What about the widow?'

'I protected her as long as she lived.'

'Under the same roof?'

'Not here, in the village . . . '

'You were intimate?'

The shopman remained silent. 'Well, she had to be protected . . . '

'How did she die?'

'I won't speak a word more – I've said everything possible; if you don't get that devil after all this, you'll share the other's fate . . . ' He suddenly sprang on the exorcist, seized him by the throat and commanded, 'Get that spirit out after getting so much out of me, otherwise . . . ' He dragged the exorcist and pushed him into the dark chamber of the shop. Thus suddenly overwhelmed, he went in howling with fright, his cry drowning the metallic clamour. As he fumbled in the dark with the shopman mounting guard at the door, the jug hit him between his legs and he let out a desperate cry, 'Ah! Alas! I'm finished,' and the cat, sensing the exit, dashed out with its metal hood on, jumped down onto the street and trotted away. The exorcist and the shopman watched in silence, staring after it. The shopman said, 'After all, it's a cat.'

'Yes, it may appear to be a cat. How do you know what is inside the cat?'

The shopman brooded and looked concerned. 'Will it visit us again?'

'Can't say,' said the exorcist. 'Call me again if there is trouble,' and made for his cubicle, saying, 'Don't worry about my *dakshina*[*] now. I can take it in the morning.'

---

[*] *dakshina*: payment, fee

Ngugi wa Thiong'o's *story is set in Kenya where the author was once detained in prison for his political opinions.*

Anya Sitaram, *who is perhaps more familiar as a television news reporter than as a writer, was born in Bombay in 1963, though she has spent most of her life in England.* Naukar *is based on real events during a year the author spent in India after leaving school.*

Separated by an ocean, Kenya and India are not dissimilar in that they were once British colonies and colonialism left its legacy in both countries.

In the next two stories, both Mrs Hill and Julia have consciences about the treatment of servants. Their 'liberal' attitudes might be well intentioned, but they have sad consequences.

The Martyr

Ngugi wa Thiong'o

When Mr and Mrs Garstone were murdered in their home by unknown gangsters, there was a lot of talk about it. It was all on the front pages of the daily papers and figured importantly in the Radio Newsreel. Perhaps this was so because they were the first European settlers to be killed in the increased wave of violence that had spread all over the country. The violence was said to have political motives. And wherever you went, in the market-places, in the Indian bazaars, in a remote African *duka*,* you were bound to hear something about the murder. There were a variety of accounts and interpretations.

Nowhere was the matter more thoroughly discussed than in a remote, lonely house built on a hill, which

* *duka*: shop

belonged, quite appropriately, to Mrs Hill. Her
husband, an old veteran settler of the pioneering
period, had died the previous year after an attack of
malaria while on a visit to Uganda. Her only son and
daughter were now getting their education at 'Home'
– home being another name for England. Being one of
the earliest settlers and owning a lot of land with big
tea plantations sprawling right across the country, she
was much respected by the others if not liked by all.

For some did not like what they considered her too
'liberal' attitude to the 'natives'. When Mrs Smiles
and Mrs Hardy came into her house two days later to
discuss the murder, they wore a look of sad triumph
– sad because Europeans (not just Mr and Mrs
Garstone) had been killed, and of triumph, because
the essential depravity and ingratitude of the
natives had been demonstrated beyond all doubt. No
longer could Mrs Hill maintain that natives could be
civilized if only they were handled in the right
manner.

Mrs Smiles was a lean, middle-aged woman whose
tough, determined nose and tight lips reminded one
so vividly of a missionary. In a sense she was.
Convinced that she and her kind formed an oasis of
civilization in a wild country of savage people, she
considered it almost her calling to keep on
reminding the natives and anyone else of the fact, by
her gait*, talk and general bearing.

Mrs Hardy was of Boer* descent and had early
migrated into the country from South Africa. Having
no opinions of her own about anything, she mostly
found herself agreeing with any views that most

*   gait: way of walking
     Boer: South African of Dutch descent

approximated to those of her husband and her race. For instance, on this day she found herself in agreement with whatever Mrs Smiles said. Mrs Hill stuck to her guns and maintained, as indeed she had always done, that the natives were obedient at heart and *all* you needed was to treat them kindly.

'That's all they need. *Treat them kindly*. They will take kindly to you. Look at my "boys". They all love me. They would do anything I ask them to!' That was her philosophy and it was shared by quite a number of the liberal, progressive type. Mrs Hill had done some liberal things for her 'boys'. Not only had she built some brick quarters (*brick*, mind you) but had also put up a school for the children. It did not matter if the school had not enough teachers or if the children learnt only half a day and worked in the plantations for the other half; it was more than most other settlers had the courage to do!

'It is horrible. Oh, a horrible act,' declared Mrs Smiles rather vehemently. Mrs Hardy agreed. Mrs Hill remained neutral.

'How could they do it? We've brought 'em civilization. We've stopped slavery and tribal wars. Were they not all leading savage miserable lives?' Mrs Smiles spoke with all her powers of oratory. Then she concluded with a sad shake of her head: 'But I've always said they'll never be civilized, simply can't take it.'

'We should show tolerance,' suggested Mrs Hill. Her tone spoke more of the missionary than Mrs Smiles' looks.

'Tolerant! Tolerant! How long shall we continue being tolerant? Who could have been more tolerant than the Garstones? Who more kind? And to think of all the squatters they maintained!'

'Well, it isn't the squatters who . . . '

'Who did? Who did?'

'They should all be hanged!' suggested Mrs Hardy. There was conviction in her voice.

'And to think they were actually called from bed by their houseboy!'

'Indeed?'

'Yes. It was their houseboy who knocked at their door and urgently asked them to open. Said some people were after him – '

'Perhaps there – '

'No! It was all planned. All a trick. As soon as the door was opened, the gang rushed in. It's all in the paper.'

Mrs Hill looked away rather guiltily. She had not read her paper.

It was time for tea. She excused herself and went near the door and called out in a kind, shrill voice.

'Njoroge! Njoroge!'

Njoroge was her 'houseboy'. He was a tall, broad-shouldered man nearing middle age. He had been in the Hills' service for more than ten years. He wore green trousers, with a red cloth-band round the waist and a red fez on his head. He now appeared at the door and raised his eyebrows in inquiry – an action which with him accompanied the words, 'Yes, Memsahib?' or 'Ndio, Bwana'.

'*Leta chai*[*].'

'Ndio, Memsahib!' and he vanished back after casting a quick glance round all the Memsahibs there assembled. The conversation which had been interrupted by Njoroge's appearance was now resumed.

'They look so innocent,' said Mrs Hardy.

'Yes. Quite the innocent flower but the serpent under it.' Mrs Smiles was acquainted with Shakespeare.

[*] *Leta chai*: Bring tea

'Been with me for ten years or so. Very faithful. Likes me very much.' Mrs Hill was defending her 'boy'.

'All the same I don't like him. I don't like his face.'

'The same with me.'

Tea was brought. They drank, still chatting about the death, the government's policy, and the political demagogues who were undesirable elements in this otherwise beautiful country. But Mrs Hill maintained that these semi-illiterate demagogues who went to Britain and thought they had education did not know the true aspirations of their people. You could still win your 'boys' by being kind to them.

Nevertheless, when Mrs Smiles and Mrs Hardy had gone, she brooded over that murder and the conversation. She felt uneasy and for the first time noticed that she lived a bit too far from any help in case of an attack. The knowledge that she had a pistol was a comfort.

Supper was over. That ended Njoroge's day. He stepped out of the light into the countless shadows and then vanished into the darkness. He was following the footpath from Mrs Hill's house to the workers' quarters down the hill. He tried to whistle to dispel the silence and loneliness that hung around him. He could not. Instead he heard a bird cry, sharp, shrill. Strange thing for a bird to cry at night.

He stopped, stood stock-still. Below, he could perceive nothing. But behind him the immense silhouette of Memsahib's house – large, imposing – could be seen. He looked back intently, angrily. In his anger, he suddenly thought he was growing old.

'You. You. I've lived with you so long. And you've reduced me to this!' Njoroge wanted to shout to the house all this and many other things that had long accumulated in his heart. The house would not respond. He felt foolish and moved on.

Again the bird cried. Twice!

'A warning to her,' Njoroge thought. And again his whole soul rose in anger – anger against those with a white skin, those foreign elements that had displaced the true sons of the land from their God-given place. Had God not promised Gekoyo* all this land, him and his children, for ever and ever? Now the land had been taken away.

He remembered his father, as he always did when these moments of anger and bitterness possessed him. He had died in the struggle – the struggle to rebuild the destroyed shrines. That was at the famous 1923 Nairobi Massacre when police fired on a people peacefully demonstrating for their rights. His father was among the people who died. Since then Njoroge had had to struggle for a living – seeking employment here and there on European farms. He had met many types – some harsh, some kind, but all dominating, giving him just what salary they thought fit for him. Then he had come to be employed by the Hills. It was a strange coincidence that he had come here. A big portion of the land now occupied by Mrs Hill was the land his father had shown him as belonging to the family. They had found the land occupied when his father and some of the others had temporarily retired to Muranga owing to famine. They had come back and *Ng'o**! the land was gone.

'Do you see that fig tree? Remember that land is yours. Be patient. Watch these Europeans. They will go and then you can claim the land.'

* Gekoyo: traditional name for the Kikuyu tribe of Kenya
  Ng'o: God

He was small then. After his father's death, Njoroge had forgotten this injunction. But when he coincidentally came here and saw the tree, he remembered. He knew it all – all by heart. He knew where every boundary went through.

Njoroge had never liked Mrs Hill. He had always resented her complacency in thinking she had done so much for the workers. He had worked with cruel types like Mrs Smiles and Mrs Hardy. But he always knew where he stood with such. But Mrs Hill! Her liberalism was almost smothering. Njoroge hated settlers. He hated above all what he thought was their hypocrisy and complacency. He knew that Mrs Hill was no exception. She was like all the others, only she loved paternalism. It convinced her she was better than the others. But she was worse. You did not know exactly where you stood with her.

All of a sudden, Njoroge shouted, 'I hate them! I hate them!' Then a grim satisfaction came over him. Tonight, anyway, Mrs Hill would die – pay for her own smug liberalism, her paternalism and pay for all the sins of her settler race. It would be one settler less.

He came to his own room. There was no smoke coming from all the other rooms belonging to the other workers. The light had even gone out in many of them. Perhaps some were already asleep or gone to the Native Reserve to drink beer. He lit the lantern and sat on the bed. It was a very small room. Sitting on the bed one could almost touch all the corners of the room if one stretched one's arms wide. Yet it was here, *here*, that he with two wives and a number of children had to live, had in fact lived for more than five years. So crammed! Yet Mrs Hill thought that she had done enough by just having the houses built with brick.

'Mzuri, sana, eh?' (very good, eh?) she was very fond of asking. And whenever she had visitors she brought them to the edge of the hill and pointed at the houses.

Again Njoroge smiled grimly to think how Mrs Hill would pay for all this self-congratulatory piety. He also knew that he had an axe to grind. He had to avenge the death of his father and strike a blow for the occupied family land. It was foresight on his part to have taken his wives and children back to the Reserve. They might else have been in the way and in any case he did not want to bring trouble to them should he be forced to run away after the act.

The other Ihii (Freedom Boys) would come at any time now. He would lead them to the house. Treacherous – yes! But how necessary.

The cry of the night bird, this time louder than ever, reached his ears. That was a bad omen. It always portended death – death for Mrs Hill. He thought of her. He remembered her. He had lived with Memsahib and Bwana for more than ten years. He knew that she had loved her husband. Of that he was sure. She almost died of grief when she had learnt of his death. In that moment her settlerism had been shorn off. In that naked moment, Njoroge had been able to pity her. Then the children! He had known them. He had seen them grow up like any other children. Almost like his own. They loved their parents, and Mrs Hill had always been so tender with them, so loving. He thought of them in England, wherever that was, fatherless and motherless.

And then he realized, too suddenly, that he could not do it. He could not tell how, but Mrs Hill had suddenly crystallized into a woman, a wife, a somebody like

Njeri or Wambui, and above all, a mother. He could not kill a woman. He could not kill a mother. He hated himself for this change. He felt agitated. He tried hard to put himself in the other condition, his former self, and see her as just a settler. As a settler, it was easy. For Njoroge hated settlers and all Europeans. If only he could see her like this (as one among many white men or settlers) then he could do it. Without scruples. But he could not bring back the other self. Not now, anyway. He had never thought of her in these terms. Until today. And yet he knew she was the same, and would be the same tomorrow – a patronizing, complacent woman. It was then he knew that he was a divided man and perhaps would ever remain like that. For now it even seemed an impossible thing to snap just like that ten years of relationship, though to him they had been years of pain and shame. He prayed and wished there had never been injustices. Then there would never have been this rift – the rift between white and black. Then he would never have been put in this painful situation.

What was he to do now? Would he betray the 'Boys'? He sat there, irresolute, unable to decide on a course of action. If only he had not thought of her in human terms! That he hated settlers was quite clear in his mind. But to kill a mother of two seemed too painful a task for him to do in a free frame of mind.

He went out.

Darkness still covered him and he could see nothing clearly. The stars above seemed to be anxiously awaiting Njoroge's decision. Then, as if their cold stare was compelling him, he began to walk, walk back to Mrs Hill's house. He had decided to save her. Then probably he would go to the forest. There, he would forever fight with a freer conscience. That seemed excellent. It would also serve as a propitiation for his betrayal of the other 'Boys'.

There was no time to lose. It was already late and the 'Boys' might come any time. So he ran with one purpose – to save the woman. At the road he heard footsteps. He stepped into the bush and lay still. He was certain that those were the 'Boys'. He waited breathlessly for the footsteps to die. Again he hated himself for this betrayal. But how could he fail to hearken to this other voice? He ran on when the footsteps had died. It was necessary to run, for if the 'Boys' discovered his betrayal he would surely meet death. But then he did not mind this. He only wanted to finish this other task first.

At last, sweating and panting, he reached Mrs Hill's house and knocked at the door, crying, 'Memsahib! Memsahib!'

Mrs Hill had not yet gone to bed. She had sat up, a multitude of thoughts crossing her mind. Ever since that afternoon's conversation with the other women, she had felt more and more uneasy. When Njoroge went and she was left alone she had gone to her safe and taken out her pistol, with which she was now toying. It was better to be prepared. It was unfortunate that her husband had died. He might have kept her company.

She sighed over and over again as she remembered her pioneering days. She and her husband and others had tamed the wilderness of this country and had developed a whole mass of unoccupied land. People like Njoroge now lived contented without a single worry about tribal wars. They had a lot to thank the Europeans for.

Yes, she did not like those politicians who came to corrupt the otherwise obedient and hard-working men, especially when treated kindly. She did not like this murder of the Garstones. No! She did not like it. And when she remembered the fact that she was really alone, she thought it might be better for her to move down to Nairobi or Kinangop and stay with friends a while. But what would she do with her boys? Leave them there? She wondered. She thought of Njoroge. A queer boy. Had he many wives? Had he a large family? It was surprising even to her to find that she had lived with him so long, yet had never thought of these things. This reflection shocked her a little. It was the first time she had ever thought of him as a man with a family. She had always seen him as a servant. Even now it seemed ridiculous to think of her houseboy as a father with a family. She sighed. This was an omission, something to be righted in future.

And then she heard a knock on the front door and a voice calling out 'Memsahib! Memsahib!'

It was Njoroge's voice. Her houseboy. Sweat broke out on her face. She could not even hear what the boy was saying for the circumstances of the Garstones' death came to her. This was her end. The end of the road. So Njoroge had led them here! She trembled and felt weak.

But suddenly, strength came back to her. She knew she was alone. She knew they would break in. No! She would die bravely. Holding her pistol more firmly in her hand, she opened the door and quickly fired. Then a nausea came over her. She had killed a man for the first time. She felt weak and fell down crying, 'Come and kill me!' She did not know that she had in fact killed her saviour.

On the following day, it was all in the papers. That a single woman could fight a gang fifty strong was bravery unknown. And to think she had killed one too!

Mrs Smiles and Mrs Hardy were especially profuse in their congratulations.

'We told you they're all bad.'

'They are all bad,' agreed Mrs Hardy. Mrs Hill kept quiet. The circumstances of Njoroge's death worried her. The more she thought about it, the more of a puzzle it was to her. She gazed still into space. Then she let out a slow enigmatic sigh.

'I don't know,' she said.

'Don't know?' Mrs Hardy asked.

'Yes. That's it. Inscrutable.' Mrs Smiles was triumphant. 'All of them should be whipped.'

'All of them should be whipped,' agreed Mrs Hardy.

Naukar[*]

Anya Sitaram

The sun beamed relentlessly on the streets of Calcutta as the rickshaw-wallah[*] toiled his way down Southern Avenue, the wooden shafts of the rickshaw rubbing against his protruding shoulder-blades and scraping away at his skin, threatening to expose his bones completely through wet, pink sores. With his thin neck straining forward, his brown hands swollen by the heat, gripping the shafts of the wagon, the rickshaw-wallah quickened his sticks of legs from an unsteady trot into a gallop and he and his livelihood careered round a bend towards Lake Gardens. Every now and again he tossed his sweating tendrils to unsettle the flies that buzzed round his head like faithful satellites. Julia Bannerjee shut her eyes as the rickshaw narrowly missed a bus, which screamed past within two inches of them. The hood of the vehicle, which had been put up to protect her from the sun, was proving to be more of a nuisance than a comfort for it was too low for her long limbs. Only if she bent double and craned her neck forward from under the hood could she see out of the jolting carriage.

If she sat upright, her vision was restricted to the rickshaw-wallah's puny waist, puny hips and thin poles of legs. She thought it was almost obscene the way his angular kneecaps, which were the widest part of his legs, jutted out.

* *naukar*: servant
   rickshaw-wallah: man who pulls a two-wheeled passenger carriage

She hated travelling by rickshaw, not only because it was uncomfortable, but also because it was painful to see a man reduced to the level of a beast as he laboured with the task of transporting another richer, fatter, more fortunate being to her destination. Rickshaw-wallahs barely lived past middle age. But if she did not travel by rickshaw, she would be depriving a man of his income, her husband had told her.

Her husband, Nilkant Bannerjee, had been a Marxist in his college days, a fine specimen of the earnest, vociferous, *khadi**-swathed intelligentsia prolific in Calcutta. Having completed his degree, he had joined Ashok Leyland and after several years had been sent to England to get some managerial experience, before returning to India to embark on more demanding tasks, including those of being a husband; for during his stay in the Midlands he had fallen in love with a tall, willowy, freckly and very fair English rose. His marriage to a foreigner had been his last act of rebellion before he succumbed to the cosy allure of affluence.

Julia had been in India for nearly a year now but had not yet grown accustomed to her new home; everything was still remarkable. Even Nilkant seemed different in his own surroundings – more arrogant, more conventional than he'd been in England. Perhaps it was just the confidence of being at home.

Sometimes she just wanted to shut herself away in a cool room and forget, for India had sharpened her awareness, exposed her senses to a bombardment of sights, smells, sounds, which terrified, amazed and sickened her. She was always apprehensive of venturing out into the roads swarming with people,

*   *khadi*: woven cotton

animals, cars, buses, trams: roads choked with chaos. She would return home trembling and exhausted after an outing, having spent her nerves and energy dodging the clutching, hungry hands of hawkers, beggars, street Romeos, all thinking a white woman easy prey. Going into the city and back to her house again involved the opening and shutting of her senses, like a wound that is never given a chance to heal but half-closed, half-dried, is ripped open again, by the thing that caused it in the first place.

Calcutta reeked of poverty, death and confusion. Everywhere buildings were crumbling into skeletal ghosts of the Raj* Beggars littered the streets, and those who were too weak to beg collapsed on the pavements and lay prone for days, while skinny stray dogs sniffed at them and people stepped over them as if avoiding rubbish, until they were fortunate enough to die or be scooped up by a Mother Teresa.

Even in the dark recesses of her own house away from the excreta, from the smell of urine, betel juice and *bidis** – India's peculiar perfume – confusion would come wafting in to invade her peace with another instalment of power cuts, so that hours were spent in primitive heat and darkness, being bitten by mosquitoes and longing for the electricity to return. When she wanted to ring a friend her phone would invariably be out of order, because some workmen digging an underground railway had accidentally cut through the cables. The authorities had been planning its construction for over ten years but every time a hole of substantial depth was made the surrounding earth would cave in and fill it up again.

---

*   Raj: the British government in India
     bidis: Indian cigarettes

'Why are they trying to build an underground,' she had asked Nilkant, 'if it's proving so dangerous? Besides there isn't enough power to light this bloody city let alone run a new railway!'

'But don't you know?' he had smiled enigmatically. 'They are building it in the hope that one day when half the population of Calcutta is underground, the electricity will fail, the soil will sink and, bingo – all our problems will be solved. No more over-crowding, no more power cuts.'

The city was a seething, multi-mouthed volcano, which spouted putrid, resentful lava at intervals and threatened to explode in a devastating eruption any day. Julia would never forget an incident within the first two weeks of her arrival when her husband and she had witnessed an accident. A street-urchin had rushed into the path of an oncoming car. It was clearly the child's fault, but the sight of the limp, bleeding five-year-old rendered lifeless by a more privileged being angered the crowd that gathered round. They grabbed hold of the driver and literally tore him limb from limb. Two deaths were reported in the *Calcutta Statesman* the next day. One was a child's and the other was a driver's who had been lynched by a mob. A crime had been committed, but hundreds of people were responsible for the driver's death. No, millions. In fact, all the poor in India were responsible.

Julia was disturbed by the sinister undercurrents that flowed beneath the fragile co-existence of rich and poor, and was puzzled by the fact that all the Indians she knew seemed unaffected. It was as if they could not see.

Julia and her rickshaw-wallah reached their destination, a grey three-storey house, a little less decrepit than the other similar structures in the higgledy-piggledy warren of residential streets. Breathing a sigh and easing herself from the sweat-soaked seat, she was seized with a sudden impulse to help the rickshaw-wallah, who was wiping his face with grim relief. So in her broken Bengali, she told him to wait and rushed through the gate and into the house.

In the kitchen, the cook was preparing *aloo paratas*[*]. Feeling awkward under his suspicious gaze, she took a couple and wrapped them in silver foil, then took a mango from the fridge in the pantry and a bottle of chilled water.

The rickshaw-wallah was squatting by his vehicle. He had poured some tobacco into his cupped left hand, which he gripped with his right hand, vigorously massaging the tobacco into a fine dust with his thumb. When he saw Julia approaching, he rose from his haunches and flicked the tobacco into his mouth.

She handed him the food, smiling, feeling gratified by her own generosity, but was a little piqued to see his unenthusiastic reception of the package at which he sullenly stared. After a few moments of embarrassed silence, Julia asked in exasperation, 'Well, what's the matter?'

'Five rupees,' he replied without lifting his eyes from the silver foil. Then Julia realized her mistake. How silly of her. She groped in her pocket, muttering apologies, feeling ridiculous as the blood throbbed in her face. Indians were lucky in that their blushes were seldom perceptible. She found a twenty-rupee note and told him to keep the change. It seemed to Julia that she had never witnessed such happiness. His sullen, haggard features were transformed by a broad

[*] *aloo paratas*: spicy potato cakes

smile as he thanked her repeatedly. The incident was sealed in her memory as one of the sunniest moments in time, all clouds and shadows far away.

Nilkant Bannerjee usually returned home after work at six o'clock each evening. He always looked forward to seeing his wife waiting for him, recently bathed, and smelling delightfully of Blue Grass, holding a restorative gin and tonic specially poured for him at exactly one minute before six o'clock. He loved to come home and find a clean bush-shirt laid on the bed by her fastidious* white hands, find the hot, sibilant shower splattering on to the white-tiled bathroom floor, on which he would stand and feel the worries of the day rinsed away. They would go out either to the Tolley Club or dinner at the Oberoi-Grand, or maybe to a lighthearted Hindi romp at an air-conditioned cinema. They usually had to go out to escape the power cuts.

Today he had a surprise for his wife as he sat down with a second drink on the batik floor cushions, which Julia had insisted on instead of a conventional sofa.

'Darling, how would you like a dog?' Nilkant knew that Julia, like all the English, worshipped dogs. He was deflated at her answer.

'But do you think it is right to have a dog in India?'

He was irritated by her persistent pangs of guilt, which dominated all her actions and soured their conversations. So he replied, 'Oh, it's all right if you give them their proper injections and keep an eye on them.' The ploy didn't work, much to his annoyance.

'You know what I mean, Nilu. Stop playing games. How can one have a dog in a country where the

* fastidious: discriminating

majority of people cannot even afford to feed themselves? How can you spend your money on an animal when it could be used to feed and clothe a sick man?'

'Very noble of you, my dear,' Nilkant said dryly, tired of always having to justify himself. 'But Suresh's labrador has had three puppies and unless we take one, it will have to be drowned. I consider that cruelty to animals.'

'I would rather a dog died than a human.'

'I thought you British would risk your lives for the salvation of your four-legged friends.' Sensing her irritation, he added in a more serious tone, 'Look, you wouldn't think twice about having a dog in England, even though you're all aware that there are people dying in the Third World.'

'That's beside the point. How can one have a pet, feed it, fawn over it, when there's a leprous beggar pushing his rotten arm through one's front gate?'

She was so persistently argumentative, Nilkant thought. But then, he remembered, he had married her more for her stimulating company than her limpid, grey eyes.

'I don't think, my sweet, that one little labrador is going to make the slightest bit of difference to the problems of the world. It's not as if we're so hard up that we'll no longer be able to give to worthier animals.' Seeing no reaction, he lost his self-control, feeling slighted that his cherished idea of several months was met with this hostile reception. He was all the more annoyed because it was her happiness that he had been considering. 'I mean, where do you draw the line? Next you'll be saying we can't have children because India's already full of famished children

suffering from rickets.' This time he knew he'd won.
She desperately wanted children.

'All right, Nilkant, you have your dog.'

Julia always awoke to the raucous song of crows,
which heralded the start of day; they hunched up
together on rooftops and windowsills, or hovered on
the stench of decaying rubbish cast out carelessly into
the street. Their calls together with the wistful cries of
hawkers floated into the bedroom, as isolated
reminders of Calcutta's teeming multitudes.

Nilkant had already left for work when Julia went
downstairs and called for breakfast. The cook came
shuffling in, smelling of onions and fish and
complained that there had been a *goonda*[*] sitting at
the gate since the crack of dawn who was refusing to
leave until the Memsahib spoke to him.

Julia peered through the half-closed shutters of the
drawing-room window and saw the *goonda* squatting
by the gate. She saw him vigorously rubbing
something in his palm with his thumb and recognised
the rickshaw-wallah.

'Well! I hope he doesn't think I'm going to give him
twenty rupees.'

She marched outside, trying to look stern, with
every intention of shooing him away. She could almost
imagine her husband's reaction. 'These people, they
are never satisfied with what they are given. Always
coming back for more.'

The little man rose to his feet, adjusting his clean
white dhoti[*], from which his skinny legs protruded,
only to be swamped in an oversized pair of black shoes.

[*]   *goonda*: layabout
      dhoti: cotton loincloth

His sunken chest was just perceptible through a starched kurta*, and in his hand was an umbrella, black and thin like one of his own limbs. She softened at the sight of him.

'I don't want to go shopping today, thank you,' she attempted in broken Bengali, but noticed that his rickshaw was nowhere in sight.

In Hindi he replied that he had come a year ago from Patna in Bihar to Calcutta after a series of misfortunes. He had been a *doodh-wallah** but his buffalo had died, his wife who had faithfully produced a son each year for the last eight years had developed a cataract in her left eye; and so he had come to Calcutta penniless in the hope of earning enough money to go back to Bihar and set up a small farm as well as pay for an eye operation. However in one year he had barely made enough to feed himself.

It did not matter if his story was untrue; it was plain that he needed help. Julia reached into her purse and produced another twenty-rupee note in the hope that he would accept it and leave. However, he shook his head and declined the money.

It was very kind of her, he explained, but what he really wanted was a job. His father had been in service, in a rich man's house and although he had not had any experience in service himself, he felt he had observed enough to be of help in any man's house.

Nilkant was furious: 'But, Julia, you can't allow a stranger into our home. You don't know anything about him!'

'I thought we needed a bearer.'

* kurta: tunic   *doodh-wallah*: milkman

Nilkant spluttered in his gin and tonic. Sometimes he felt there was an invisible wall between himself and his wife, in spite of all the barriers they had leapt to cement their relationship. She knew very well that the cook, an old retainer from his mother's house in Alipur, was responsible for selecting servants. How could an inexperienced girl from England be any kind of judge? Her pig-headedness baffled him.

'Sack him. I'm not having him in this house.'

'But you haven't even seen him. You'll agree with me, when you see him.' As usual, she was calmer than him and this only served to increase his anger, which swelled like a balloon inside his head pushing out all reason. He could hardly speak.

'You're mad.' For a moment his anger subsided as he remembered their conversation the previous evening. But then it rose again, triumphant, for he felt he understood her.

'Miss Benevolent has undertaken to solve the problems of the world by folding her downy wings round a rickshaw-wallah who says he's a bankrupt milkman, the son of a noble bearer. Let everyone follow her divine example. Love thy neighbour regardless of the fact that he's a worthless rogue. Then everyone in the world will be happy, except yourself, because your cherished object of charity has run off with all your worldly goods. For God's sake, Julia, have some sense!'

'I can't just ignore poverty when it is glaring me in the face. Just grant me this one happiness.'

Nilkant was faintly reminded of his own argument the evening before. The acquisition of a pet ultimately meant enhancing one's own happiness, but he had been unable to express it in front of Julia, her idea of happiness being somewhat different. And now he was tired – he hated the recent uneasiness that had descended between them like a damp mist, leaving a sad trail of confusion in their midst. She would have her rickshaw-wallah, he had his dog.

Afterwards, whenever friends came to dinner and remarked on the quaint bearer in the crisply starched dhoti and kurta and shiny black shoes, he could not resist drawing a parallel between the puppy that gnawed at the furniture and the bearer who served the drinks: the only drawback was that it was slightly more dangerous to keep a man as a pet than a dog.

Gradually Julia was becoming accustomed to her new life in Calcutta. The dreams of England she had frequently dreamed on first arriving – its green fields, vital freshness, comfort, peace and quiet – ceased to haunt her and she began to dream of Calcutta, her Indian friends. The heat, the dust, the din, the dirt, the smells, the crowds, the flies and the dying were no longer as startling. She no longer thought of the bearer as an impoverished rickshaw-wallah, but as a curio (the result of her English eccentricity Nilkant would tell everyone). Yet even though the bearer was often clumsy, inept at serving drinks and despised by the other servants, she insisted on keeping him, for she felt that she could detect a goodness in him, like an enduring metal, which others failed to see.

On their first wedding anniversary, her mother-in-law gave her a necklace, heavy with gold, diamonds, emeralds and rubies. In England her only jewellery of any distinction had been a string of cultured pearls. She would have balked at wearing anything richer, but in India such a necklace only merged into inconspicuousness with the many gold-encrusted silks and sparkling jewels. She thought it looked gaudy on her austere, white neck, but refusing to wear it would prove to be another source of discord between her husband and herself. She would do her utmost to prevent another spell of unpleasantness, the previous episodes still lingering in the air like stale smoke.

Far from being an object of charity, the rickshaw-wallah had been elevated to a symbol of her own sound judgement. To hear him reproached was like receiving criticisms of herself.

One day he disappeared and was nowhere to be seen for several days. Julia had to contend with the cook's supercilious* glare and Nilkant's inevitable exclamations of delight, 'See what I told you! The man is totally unreliable,' all of which served to crumble her self-esteem, making her sullen and irritable.

'I can't stand the way the cook behaves towards me!' she told Nilkant, but he was not sympathetic.

'It's all a figment of your imagination. He behaves like he has always done. It's only because you're feeling foolish yourself, that you think everyone is mocking you.'

She rebelled by refusing to be sociable in the evenings during those few days when the rickshaw-wallah was away. No gin and tonic was waiting for Nilkant when he returned home from work, because it had been the bearer's job and Julia pretended each evening that she had forgotten to pour it. Nilkant went to the club alone, for Julia said she was tired after running the house all day without proper assistance. So while he sat playing bridge at increasingly high stakes, she sat reading Rabindranath Tagore* by the

---

* supercilious: superior
  Rabindranath Tagore: Indian poet

light of a paraffin lamp, sweating abundantly and being bitten by mosquitoes.

Julia was in no mood to conceal her triumph when the rickshaw-wallah returned a week later, his shadowed eye-sockets blackened further by bruises. His nose had been broken.

'You who have no faith!' she would be heard sighing, 'And the poor man was knocked off his bicycle by a truck! Just imagine while he was lying bleeding and neglected in some gutter, you were condemning him for his inconstancy and deviousness. You who have no faith!'

Her self-esteem, which had been squashed in the last week, rose to new and excessive heights. Julia continued to rebel. One night when Nilkant and herself were to dine at his parents' house and she had been expected to dress appropriately, she belligerently refused and wrenched off her necklace, when Nilkant's back was turned, leaving it glittering provocatively on the bed.

It was gone. The discovery knocked her breath away and she had to sit on the bed while the room span round her, until her breath came back in short, agitated pants. Panic welled inside her. She tore the sheets off the bed, crawled on hands and knees on the cold stone floor, searching for non-existent crevices, then feeling a heavy sickness clogging the pit of her stomach, she began to rummage through the drawers, scattering the contents all over the room, all the time muttering, 'O my God! O my God!' under her breath, until Nilkant found her with dishevelled hair and terrified, dilated eyes, peering into the night.

'He couldn't have taken it. He's sitting downstairs looking perfectly innocent. It could have been the cook, the *dhobi**, an intruder, but Christ, not him!' Seeing Nilkant's severe face, she started to cry. 'Don't call the police,' she pleaded between sobs, 'we can question him ourselves.' She reached for his hand but he flinched at her touch.

'He deserves to be whipped. That necklace had been in our family for years. It's priceless. If anything has happened to it –'

'But you're saying he's guilty even before he's proved.'

'Of course he's guilty. It's obvious.' He clenched his fist. 'The man mysteriously disappears for seven days and comes back covered in bruises. He's in trouble and needs money. So at the first opportunity he steals.'

'But he'd be stupid to steal something like that.'

'He's a desperate man.'

'Well, we should help him then.' Julia realized that she was also talking as if his guilt was a proven fact.

Her remark further enraged Nilkant who blurted out, 'You're such a perverse little idiot. For what shallow reasons did you remove that necklace when you should have worn it to my parents' house?'

For a day the house was besieged by hordes of policemen, all intent on combing through the Bannerjees' belongings, sniffing under the furniture, or standing with expressions of great authority on their faces, but in fact having little to do or say.

The Chief Inspector, less unsavoury looking than his helpers, who would have been frightening to meet on a dark night, twirled his swashbuckling moustache in thought and asked questions such as: 'But if you

* *dhobi*: laundryman

please, Madam, where exactly on the bed did you deposit this necklace?' or: 'But please, Madam, why did you remove it before going out?'

Julia became more and more flustered.

Nilkant did not help either. It was as if he was inflicting his last triumphant revenge on her for having employed the rickshaw-wallah against his will. At intervals he came and sat beside her, listening to the questions, and when the police left, he said, 'I have told them about the man's suspicious behaviour,' as if he were doing her a favour.

As soon as the police set eyes on the rickshaw-wallah, having interrogated the indignant cook and cleaning woman, who all threatened to leave because of the insult to their good names, they knew they had their man. He was taken away for questioning. For three days he refused to admit to the crime, but as the beatings became more persistent he gave in.

'You see, Julia,' Nilkant concluded, 'he was rotten through and through. Never think that these people will be grateful. They're just out to grab as much as they can get.'

Julia was not convinced. 'If only I hadn't left my necklace there, the poor man wouldn't have been tempted.'

For a while she was wracked by guilt. Because of her the rickshaw-wallah was now subjected to worse hardships than he could ever have known. She shuddered as she remembered the chilling stories of police brutality.

As the weeks passed, the episode was gradually consigned to hazy memory, no longer her dominant thought, as the reassuring routine of the present took over. One day when the incident was all but forgotten, the Chief Inspector rang. 'Madam, we've found your necklace,' he declared.

Julia could have cried with relief, 'Oh, thank Goodness! Where did he hide it?'

There was a long silence. 'It wasn't hidden, Madam.' The policeman paused again. 'We found it while arresting a notorious burglar who we've been hunting for several months. It looks as if it was he who committed the theft. The bearer has been released.'

'Are you sure . . . that it wasn't him?'

'Yes, Madam, quite certain. Apparently the real thief was disturbed while committing the burglary. All he had time to take was the first thing that he could find. That was the necklace on the bed.'

Putting the receiver back, Julia moved unsteadily to the window, taking long, deep breaths. Outside the night was inky black. The man was free – but she felt not a flicker of relief. Just numbness. From the neighbouring buildings emerged a concert of blaring televisions. A strong breeze wafted past her, hot, oppressive.

Suddenly Julia felt the beads of sweat prick her face. She had caught sight of something. An outline against the darkness – it appeared to move. At the gate she could make out a figure. Her heart beating loudly, she strained her eyes transfixed, unable to look away. And as she stared a pair of dark eyes met hers.

——————— Heat and Dust ———————

Samuel Selvon *was born in 1923 in Trinidad, where* A Drink of Water *from his short story anthology* Ways of Sunlight *is set. The son of an East Indian father and a half-Scottish mother, Selvon always thought of himself as Trinidadian and a part of the Creole culture which developed from the fusing into one society of a mixture of different nationalities. Samuel Selvon died in 1994.*

Bessie Head *was born in South Africa in 1937. She was the child of a racially mixed family, her father being black, her mother white. This caused her problems under the South African apartheid system and in 1964 Bessie Head moved to Botswana, where she lived in the village of Serowe.* Looking for a Rain God *is one of the stories in her collection,* The Collector of Treasures, *and is set in Botswana. Bessie Head died in 1986.*

Both of these stories are set in rural areas where conditions are harsh, and survival is a constant battle against hostile elements. The writers examine their characters' responses to the moral dilemmas they have to face during extreme conditions of drought and suffering.

A Drink of Water

Samuel Selvon

The time when the rains didn't come for three months and the sun was a yellow furnace in the sky was known as the Great Drought in Trinidad. It happened when everyone was expecting the sky to burst open with rain to fill the dry streams and water the parched earth.

But each day was the same; the sun rose early in a blue sky, and all day long the farmers lifted their eyes, wondering what had happened to Parjanya, the rain god. They rested on their hoes and forks and wrung perspiration from their clothes, seeing no hope in labour, terrified by the thought that if no rain fell soon they would lose their crops and livestock and face starvation and death.

In the tiny village of Las Lomas, out in his vegetable garden, Manko licked dry lips and passed a wet sleeve over his dripping face. Somewhere in the field a cow mooed mournfully, sniffing around for a bit of green in the cracked earth. The field was a desolation of drought. The trees were naked and barks peeled off trunks as if they were diseased. When the wind blew, it was heavy and unrelieving, as if the heat had taken all the spirit out of it. But Manko still opened his shirt and turned his chest to it when it passed.

He was a big man, grown brown and burnt from years of working on the land. His arms were bent and he had a crouching position even when he stood upright. When he laughed he showed more tobacco stain than teeth.

But Manko had not laughed for a long time. Bush fires had swept Las Lomas and left the garden plots charred and smoking. Cattle were dropping dead in the heat. There was scarcely any water in the village; the river was dry with scummy mud. But with patience one could collect a bucket of water. Boiled, with a little sugar to make it drinkable, it had to do.

Sometimes, when the children knew that someone had gone to the river for water, they hung about in the village main road waiting with bottles and calabash shells, and they fell upon the water-carrier as soon as he hove in sight.

'Boil the water first before drinking!' was the warning cry. But even so two children were dead and many more were on the sick list, their parents too poor to seek medical aid in the city twenty miles away.

Manko sat in the shade of a mango tree and tried to look on the bright side of things. Such a dry season meant that the land would be good for corn seeds when the rains came. He and his wife Rannie had been working hard and saving money with the hope of sending Sunny, their son, to college in the city.

Rannie told Manko: 'We poor, and we ain't have no education, but is all right, we go get old soon and dead, and what we have to think about is the boy. We must let him have plenty learning and come a big man in Trinidad.'

And Manko, proud of his son, used to boast in the evening, when the villagers got together to talk and smoke, that one day Sunny would be a lawyer or a doctor.

But optimism was difficult now. His livestock was dying out, and the market was glutted with yams. He had a great pile in the yard which he could not sell.

Manko took a look at his plot of land and shook his head. There was no sense in working any more today. He took his cutlass and hoe and calabash shell which had a string so he could hold it dangling. He shook it, and realised with burning in his throat that it was empty, though he had left a few mouthfuls in it. He was a fool; he should have known that the heat would dry it up if he took it out in the garden with him. He licked his lips and, shouldering the tools, walked slowly down the winding path which led to his hut.

Rannie was cooking in the open fireplace in the yard. Sunny was sitting under the poui* tree, but when he saw his father he ran towards him and held the calabash shell eagerly. Always when Manko returned from the fields he brought back a little water for his son. But this time he could only shake his head.

'Who went for water today by the river?' he asked Rannie.

* poui: the national tree of Trinidad – pink or yellow

'I think was Jagroop,' she answered, stirring the pot with a large wooden spoon, 'but he ain't coming back till late.'

She covered the pot and turned to him. 'Tomorrow we going to make offering for rain,' she said.

Next day, Las Lomas held a big feast, and prayers were said to the rain god, Parjanya. And then two days later, a man called Rampersad struck water in a well he had been digging for weeks. It was the miracle they had been praying for. That day everyone drank their fill, and Rampersad allowed each villager a bucket of water, and Manko told Sunny: 'See how blessing doesn't only come from up the sky, it does come from the earth, too.'

Rampersad's wife was a selfish and crafty woman, and while the villagers were filling their buckets she stood by the doorway of their hut and watched them. That night she told her husband he was a fool to let them have the water for nothing.

'They have money hide up,' she urged him. 'They could well pay for it. The best thing to do is to put barb' wire all round the well, and set a watchdog to keep guard in the night so nobody thief the water. Then say you too poor to give away for nothing. Charge a dollar for a bucket and two shillings for half-bucket. We make plenty money and come rich.'

When Rampersad announced this, the villagers were silent and aghast that a man could think of such a scheme when the whole village was burning away in the drought, and two children had died.

Rampersad bought a shotgun and said he would shoot anyone he found trespassing on his property. He put up the barbed wire and left a ferocious watchdog near the well at nights.

As April went, there was still no sign in the sky. In Las Lomas, the villagers exhausted their savings in buying Rampersad's water to keep alive.

Manko got up one morning and looked in the tin under his bed in which he kept his money. There was enough for just two buckets of water. He said to Rannie: 'How long could you make two buckets of water last, if we use it only for drinking?'

'That is all the money remaining?' Rannie looked at him with fear.

He nodded and looked outside where the poui tree had begun to blossom. 'Is a long time now,' he said softly, 'a long time, too long. It can't last. The rain will fall, just don't be impatient.'

Rannie was not impatient, but thirst made her careless. It happened soon after the two buckets were empty. She forgot to boil a pan of river water, and only after she had drunk a cupful did she realise her fatal mistake. She was afraid to tell Manko; she kept silent about the incident.

Next day, she could not get out of bed. She rolled and tossed as fever ravaged her body.

Manko's eyes were wide with fright when he saw the signs of fever. Sunny, who had not been to school for weeks, wanted to do whatever he could, anything at all, to get his mother well so she could talk and laugh and cook again.

He spoke to his father after Rannie had fallen into a fitful sleep, with perspiration soaking through the thin white sheet.

'No money remaining for water, *bap**?'

Manko shook his head.

'And no money for doctor or medicine?'

*   *bap*: father

He shook his head again.

'But how it is this man Rampersad have so much water and we ain't have any? Why don't we just go and take it?'

'The water belong to Rampersad,' Manko said. 'Is his own, and if he choose to sell it, is his business. We can't just go and take, that would be thiefing. You must never thief from another man, Sunny. That is a big, big, sin. No matter what happen.'

'But is not a fair thing,' the boy protested, digging his hands into the brittle soil. 'If we had clean water, we could get *mai** better, not so?'

'Yes, *beta*,*' Manko sighed and rose to his feet. 'You stay and mind *mai*, I going to try and get some river water.'

All day, Sunny sat in the hut brooding over the matter, trying hard to understand why his mother should die from lack of water when a well was filled in another man's yard.

It was late in the evening when Manko returned. As he had expected, the river was nearly dry, a foul trickle of mud not worth drinking. He found the boy quiet and moody. After a while, Sunny went out.

Manko was glad to be alone. He didn't want Sunny to see him leaving the hut later in the night, with the bucket and the rope. It would be difficult to explain that he was stealing Rampersad's water only because it was a matter of life or death.

He waited impatiently for Rannie to fall asleep. It seemed she would never close her eyes. She just turned and twisted restlessly, and once she looked at him and asked if rain had fallen, and he put his rough hand on her hot forehead and said softly no, but that he had

---

*　*mai*: mother　　*beta*: child

seen a sign that evening, a great black cloud low down in the east.

Then suddenly her fever rose again, and she was delirious. This time he could not understand what she said. She was moaning in a queer, strangled way.

It was midnight before she fell into a kind of swoon, a red flush on her face. Manko knew what he must do now. He stood looking at her, torn between the fear of leaving her and the desperate plan that he had made. She might die while he was gone, and yet – he must try it.

He frowned as he went out and saw the moon like a night sun in the sky, lighting up the village. He turned to the east and his heart leapt as he saw the cloud moving towards the village in a slow breeze. It seemed so far away, and it was moving as if it would take days to get over the fields. Perhaps it would; perhaps it would change direction and go scudding down into the west, and not a drop of water.

He moved off towards the well, keeping behind the huts and deep into the trees. It took him ten minutes to get near the barbed wire fence, and he stood in the shadow of a giant silk-cotton tree. He leaned against the trunk and drew in his breath sharply as his eyes discerned a figure on the other side of the well, outside the barbed wire.

The figure stopped, as though listening, then began clambering over the fence.

Even as he peered to see if he could recognize who it was, a sudden darkness fell as the cloud swept over the moon in the freshening wind.

Manko cast his eyes upwards swiftly, and when he looked down again the figure was on the brink of the well, away from the sleeping watchdog.

It was a great risk to take; it was the risk Manko himself had to take. But this intrusion upset his plan. He could not call out; the slightest sound would wake the dog, and what it did not do to the thief, Rampersad would do with his shotgun.

For a moment, Manko's heart failed him. He smelt death very near – for the unknown figure at the well, and for himself, too. He had been a fool to come. Then a new frenzy seized him. He remembered the cruel red flush on Rannie's cheeks when he had left her. Let her die happy, if a drop of water could make her so. Let her live, if a drop of water could save her. His own thirst flared in his throat; how much more she must be suffering!

He saw the bucket slide noiselessly down and the rope paid out. Just what he had planned to do. Now draw it up, cautiously, yes, and put it to rest gently on the ground. Now kneel and take a drink, and put the fire out in your body. For God's sake, why didn't the man take a drink? What was he waiting for? Ah, that was it, but be careful, do not make the slightest noise, or everything will be ruined. Bend your head down . . .

Moonrays shot through a break in the cloud and lit up the scene.

It was Sunny.

'*Beta!*' Before he could think, the startled cry had left Manko's lips.

The dog sprang up at the sound and moved with uncanny swiftness. Before Sunny could turn, it had sprung across the well, straight at the boy's throat.

Manko scrambled over the fence, ripping away his clothes and drawing blood. He ran and cleared the well in a great jump, and tried to tear the beast away from the struggling boy. The dog turned, growling low in the throat as it faced this new attacker.

Manko stumbled and fell, breathing heavily. He felt teeth sink into his shoulder and he bit his lip hard to keep from screaming in pain.

Suddenly the dog was wrenched away as Sunny joined the fight. The boy put his arms around the dog's neck and jerked it away from his father with such force that when the animal let go they both fell rolling to the ground.

Manko flung out his arm as he sprang up. In doing so, he capsized the bucket of water with a loud clang. Even in the struggle for life he could not bear to see the earth sucking up the water like a sponge. In fear and fury, he snatched the empty bucket and brought it down with all his strength on the dog's head.

The animal gave a whimper and rolled off the boy and lay still.

'Who that, thiefing my water?' Rampersad came running out into the yard, firing his shotgun wildly in the air.

'Quick, boy! Over the fence!' Manko grabbed the bucket and tossed it over. He almost threw Sunny to safety as the boy faltered on the wire. Then he half-dragged his own bleeding body up, and fell exhausted on the other side.

Sunny put his arm under his father and helped him up. Together they ran into the shadow of the trees.

The noise of the gun and Rampersad's yells had wakened the whole village, and everyone was astir.

Father and son hid the bucket in a clump of dry bush and, waiting for a minute to recover themselves, joined the crowd which was gathering in front of Rampersad's hut.

Rampersad was beside himself with rage. He threatened them all with jail, screaming that he would find out who had stolen the water and killed the dog.

'Who is the thief? You catch him?' The crowd jeered and booed. 'It damn good. Serve you right.' Clutching his father's arm tightly, Sunny danced and chuckled with delight at Rampersad's discomfiture.

But suddenly silence and darkness fell together. A large black blob of cloud blotted out the moon. The sky was thick with clouds piling up on each other and there was a new coolness in the wind.

As one, the crowd knelt and prayed to the rain god. The sky grew black; it looked as if the moon had never been there. For hours they prayed, until Manko, thinking of Rannie, gently tapped his son and beckoned him away. They walked home hand in hand.

It was Sunny who felt the first drop. It lay on his hand like a diamond shining in the dark.

'Bap?' He raised questioning eyes to his father. 'Look!'

As Manko looked up, another drop fell on his face and rolled down his cheek. The wind became stronger; there was a swift fall of some heavy drops. Then the wind died like a sigh. A low rumble in the east; then silence. Perhaps Parjanya was having a joke with them, perhaps there would be no rain after all.

And then it came sweeping in from the north-east, with a rising wind. Not very heavy at first, but in thrusts, coming and going. They opened their mouths and laughed, and water fell in. They shouted and cried and laughed again.

Manko approached the hut where Rannie lay, and he was trembling at what he would find. He said to the boy: '*Beta*. You stay here. I go in first to see *mai*.' The boy's face went rigid with sudden fear. Though he was already drenched to the skin, he took shelter under the poui tree in the yard.

Manko was hardly inside the door when he gave a sharp cry of alarm. He thought he saw a ghostly figure tottering towards him, its face luminous-grey. He flattened himself against the wall and closed his eyes. It was cruel of the gods to torment him like this. This was not Rannie: Rannie was lying in bed in the next room, she could not be alive any more.

'Manko.' It was her voice, and yet it was not her voice. 'What noise is that I hear? Is rain?'

He could not speak. Slowly, he forced himself to stretch out his hand and touch her forehead. It felt cold and unnatural.

He withdrew his hand, and began to tremble uncontrollably.

'Manko,' the lips formed the words. 'Manko, give me water!'

Something fell to the floor with a clatter. He saw that it was a tin cup, and that she had been holding it in her hand. She swayed towards him, and he caught her. Then Manko knew that it was a miracle. Rannie was shaking with cold and weakness, but the fever was gone, and she was alive.

Realization burst upon him with such force that he almost fainted.

He muttered: 'I will get some for you.'

He picked up the cup and ran out into the lashing rain. Sunny, watching from the poui tree, was astonished to see his father standing motionless in the downpour. He had taken off his shirt, and his bare back and chest were shining with water. His face, uplifted to the sky, was the face of a man half-crazy with joy. He might be laughing or crying, Sunny could not tell; and his cheeks were streaming, perhaps with tears, perhaps with Parjanya's rain.

Looking for a Rain God
Bessie Head

It is lonely at the lands where the people go to plough. These lands are vast clearings in the bush, and the wild bush is lonely too. Nearly all the lands are within walking distance from the village. In some parts of the bush where the underground water is very near the surface, people made little rest camps for themselves and dug shallow wells to quench their thirst while on their journey to their own lands. They experienced all kinds of things once they left the village. They could rest at shady watering places full of lush, tangled trees with delicate pale-gold and purple wild flowers springing up between soft green moss and the children could hunt around for wild figs and any berries that might be in season. But from 1958, a seven-year drought fell upon the land and even the watering places began to look as dismal as the dry open thorn-bush country; the leaves of the trees curled up and withered; the moss became dry and hard and, under the shade of the tangled trees, the ground turned a powdery black and white, because there was no rain. People said rather humorously that if you tried to catch the rain in a cup it would only fill a teaspoon. Towards the beginning of the seventh year of drought, the summer had become an anguish to live through. The air was so dry and moisture-free that it burned the skin. No one knew what to do to escape the heat and tragedy was in the air. At the beginning of that summer, a number of men just went out of their homes and hung themselves to death from trees. The majority of the people had lived off crops, but for two years past they had all returned from the lands with only their rolled-up skin blankets and cooking utensils. Only the charlatans[*], incanters[*], and witch-doctors made a pile of money during this time because people were always turning to them in desperation for little talismans and herbs to rub on the plough for the crops to grow and the rain to fall.

The rains were late that year. They came in early November, with a promise of good rain. It wasn't the full, steady downpour of the years of good rain, but thin, scanty, misty rain. It softened the earth and a rich growth of green things sprang up everywhere for the animals to eat. People were called to the village *kgotla*[*] to hear the proclamation of the beginning of the ploughing season; they stirred themselves and whole families began to move off to the lands to plough.

The family of the old man, Mokgobja, were among those who left early for the lands. They had a donkey cart and piled everything on to it. Mokgobja – who was over seventy years old; two little girls, Neo and Boseyong; their mother Tiro and an unmarried sister, Nesta; and the father and supporter of the family, Ramadi, who drove the donkey cart. In the rush of the first hope of rain, the man, Ramadi, and the two women, cleared the land of thorn-bush and then hedged their vast ploughing area with this same thorn-bush to protect the future crop from the goats they had brought along for milk. They cleared out and deepened the old well with its pool of muddy water and still in this light, misty rain, Ramadi inspanned two oxen and turned the earth over with a hand plough.

[*]   charlatans: fraudsters   incanters: makers of spells
    kgotla: assembly of tribal elders

The land was ready and ploughed, waiting for the crops. At night, the earth was alive with insects singing and rustling about in search of food. But suddenly, by mid-November, the rain fled away; the rain-clouds fled away and left the sky bare. The sun danced dizzily in the sky, with a strange cruelty. Each day the land was covered in a haze of mist as the sun sucked up the last drop of moisture out of the earth. The family sat down in despair, waiting and waiting. Their hopes had run so high; the goats had started producing milk, which they had eagerly poured on their porridge, now they ate plain porridge with no milk. It was impossible to plant the corn, maize, pumpkin and water-melon seeds in the dry earth. They sat the whole day in the shadow of the huts and even stopped thinking, for the rain had fled away. Only the children, Neo and Boseyong, were quite happy in their little girl world. They carried on with their game of making house like their mother and chattered to each other in light, soft tones. They made children from sticks around which they tied rags, and scolded them severely in an exact imitation of their own mother. Their voices could be heard scolding the day long: 'You stupid thing, when I send you to draw water, why do you spill half of it out of the bucket!' 'You stupid thing! Can't you mind the porridge-pot without letting the porridge burn!' And then they would beat the rag-dolls on their bottoms with severe expressions.

The adults paid no attention to this; they did not even hear the funny chatter; they sat waiting for rain; their nerves were stretched to breaking-point willing the rain to fall out of the sky. Nothing was important, beyond that. All their animals had been sold during the bad years to purchase food, and of all their herd only two goats were left. It was the women of the family who finally broke down under the strain of waiting for rain. It was really the two women who caused the death of the little girls. Each night they started a weird, high-pitched wailing that began on a low, mournful note and whipped up to a frenzy. Then they would stamp their feet and shout as though they had lost their heads. The men sat quiet and self-controlled; it was important for men to maintain their self-control at all times but their nerve was breaking too. They knew the women were haunted by the starvation of the coming year.

Finally, an ancient memory stirred in the old man, Mokgobja. When he was very young and the customs of the ancestors still ruled the land, he had been witness to a rain-making ceremony. And he came alive a little, struggling to recall the details which had been buried by years and years of prayer in a Christian church. As soon as the mists cleared a little, he began consulting in whispers with his youngest son, Ramadi. There was, he said, a certain rain god who accepted only the sacrifice of the bodies of children. Then the rain would fall; then the crops would grow, he said. He explained the ritual and as he talked, his memory became a conviction and he began to talk with unshakeable authority. Ramadi's nerves were smashed by the nightly wailing of the women and soon the two men began whispering with the two women. The children continued their game: 'You stupid thing! How could you have lost the money on the way to the shop! You must have been playing again!'

After it was all over and the bodies of the two little girls had been spread across the land, the rain did not fall. Instead, there was a deathly silence at night and the devouring heat of the sun by day. A terror, extreme and deep, overwhelmed the whole family. They packed, rolling up their skin blankets and pots, and fled back to the village.

People in the village soon noted the absence of the two little girls. They had died at the lands and were buried there, the family said. But people noted their ashen, terror-stricken faces and a murmur arose. What had killed the children, they wanted to know? And the family replied that they had just died. And people said amongst themselves that it was strange that the two deaths had occurred at the same time. And there was a feeling of great unease at the unnatural looks of the family. Soon the police came around. The family told them the same story of death and burial at the lands. They did not know what the children had died of. So the police asked to see the graves. At this, the mother of the children broke down and told everything.

Throughout that terrible summer the story of the children hung like a dark cloud of sorrow over the village, and the sorrow was not assuaged when the old man and Ramadi were sentenced to death for ritual murder. All they had on the statute books was that ritual murder was against the law and must be stamped out with the death penalty. The subtle story of strain and starvation and breakdown was inadmissible evidence in court; but all the people who lived off crops knew in their hearts that only a hair's breadth had saved them from sharing a fate similar to that of the Mokgobja family. They could have killed something to make the rain fall.

Betrayal

Nadine Gordimer *was born in 1923 in the Transvaal in South Africa. A strong opponent of South African apartheid, she once wrote: 'I feel inadequate as a human being in my situation as a white South African, but as a writer I think I have arrived at a stage through my work where if I write about blacks or I create black characters, I feel I have the right to do so. I know enough to do so.'* (London Magazine) *She has been awarded many literary prizes and honours, including the Booker Prize and, in 1991, the Nobel Prize for Literature.*

Seema Jena *came to England in 1988 on a Commonwealth Scholarship after graduating from Madras University. Her story* In Another World *won the national competition for Black British writers.*

Alice Walker, *an African American, was born in Georgia in 1944. A strong advocate of equal rights for black people, she was, for many years, very active in the American civil rights movement. She has written poetry, short stories and novels, and her novel* The Color Purple *was made into a film by Steven Spielberg.*

These three stories, from South Africa, India and the United States of America, examine various aspects of betrayal in relationships. The characters are capable not only of betraying, sometimes deliberately, sometimes unconsciously, the feelings of people close to them, but also their own integrity.

Country Lovers

Nadine Gordimer

The farm children play together when they are small; but once the white children go away to school they soon don't play together any more, even in the holidays. Although most of the black children get some sort of schooling, they drop every year further behind the grades passed by the white children; the childish vocabulary, the child's exploration of the adventurous possibilities of dams, koppies[*], mealie lands[*] and veld[*] – there comes a time when the white children have surpassed these with the vocabulary of boarding-school and the possibilities of inter-school sports matches and the kind of adventures seen at the cinema. This usefully coincides with the age of twelve or thirteen; so that by the time early adolescence is reached, the black children are making, along with the bodily changes common to all, an easy transition to adult forms of address, beginning to call their old playmates 'miss' and *'baasie'*, little master.

The trouble was Paulus Eysendyck did not seem to realize that Thebedi was now simply one of the crowd of farm children down at the kraal[*], recognizable in his sister's old clothes. The first Christmas holidays after he had gone to boarding-school he brought home for Thebedi a painted box he had made in his woodwork class. He had to give it to her secretly because he had nothing for the other children, at the kraal. And she gave him, before he went back to school, a bracelet she had made of thin brass wire and the grey-and-white beans of the castor oil crop his father cultivated. (When they used to play together, she was the one who had taught Paulus how to make clay oxen for their toy spans[*].) There was a craze, even in the *platteland*[*] towns like the one where he was at school, for boys to wear elephant hair and other bracelets beside their watch-straps; his was admired, friends asked him to get similar ones for them. He said the natives made them on his father's farm and he would try.

---

*   koppies: small hills   mealie lands: maize fields
    veld: grassland   kraal: tribal village
    spans: yoked pairs of oxen
    platteland: remote, undeveloped area

When he was fifteen, six feet tall, and tramping round at school dances with the girls from the 'sister' school in the same town; when he had learnt how to tease and flirt and fondle quite intimately these girls who were the daughters of prosperous farmers like his father; when he had even met one who, at a wedding he had attended with his parents on a nearby farm, had let him do with her in a locked storeroom what people did when they made love – when he was as far from his childhood as all this, he still brought home from a shop in town a red plastic belt and gilt hoop earrings for the black girl, Thebedi. She told her father the missus had given these to her as a reward for some work she had done – it was true she sometimes was called to help out in the farmhouse. She told the girls in the kraal that she had a sweetheart nobody knew about, far away, away on another farm, and they giggled, and teased, and admired her. There was a boy in the kraal called Njabulo who said he wished he could have bought her a belt and earrings.

When the farmer's son was home for the holidays she wandered far from the kraal and her companions. He went for walks alone. They had not arranged this; it was an urge each followed independently. He knew it was she, from a long way off. She knew that his dog would not bark at her. Down at the dried-up river-bed where five or six years ago the children had caught a *leguaan** one great day – a creature that combined ideally the size and ferocious aspect of the crocodile with the harmlessness of the lizard – they squatted side by side on the earth bank. He told her travellers' tales: about school, about the punishments at school, particularly, exaggerating both their nature and his

* *leguaan*: iguana

indifference to them. He told her about the town of
Middleburg, which she had never seen. She had
nothing to tell but she prompted with many questions,
like any good listener. While he talked he twisted and
tugged at the roots of white stinkwood* and Cape
willow trees that looped out of the eroded earth around
them. It had always been a good spot for children's
games, down there hidden by the mesh of old,
ant-eaten trees held in place by vigorous ones, wild
asparagus bushing up between the trunks, and here
and there prickly pear cactus sunken-skinned and
bristly, like an old man's face, keeping alive sapless
until the next rainy season. She punctured the dry
hide of a prickly pear again and again with a sharp
stick while she listened. She laughed a lot at what he
told her, sometimes dropping her face on her knees,
sharing amusement with the cool shady earth beneath
her bare feet. She put on her pair of shoes – white
sandals, thickly Blanco-ed against the farm dust –
when he was on the farm, but these were taken off and
laid aside, at the river-bed. One summer afternoon
when there was water flowing there and it was very
hot she waded in as they used to do when they were
children, her dress bunched modestly and tucked into
the legs of her pants. The schoolgirls he went
swimming with at dams or pools on neighbouring
farms wore bikinis but the sight of their dazzling
bellies and thighs in the sunlight had never made him
feel what he felt now, when the girl came up the bank
and sat beside him, the drops of water beading off her
dark legs the only points of light in the earth-smelling,
deep shade. They were not afraid of one another, they
had known one another always; he did with her what

* stinkwood: species of laurel with an unpleasant smell

he had done that time in the storeroom at the wedding, and this time it was so lovely, so lovely, he was surprised . . . and she was surprised by it, too – he could see in her dark face that was part of the shade, with her big dark eyes, shiny as soft water, watching him attentively: as she had when they used to huddle over their teams of mud oxen, as she had when he told her about detention weekends at school.

They went to the river-bed often through those summer holidays. They met just before the light went, as it does quite quickly, and each returned home with the dark – she to her mother's hut, he to the farmhouse – in time for the evening meal. He did not tell her about school or town any more. She did not ask questions any longer. He told her, each time, when they would meet again. Once or twice it was very early in the morning; the lowing of the cows being driven to graze came to them where they lay, dividing them with unspoken recognition of the sound read in their two pairs of eyes, opening so close to each other.

He was a popular boy at school. He was in the second, then the first soccer team. The head girl of the 'sister' school was said to have a crush on him; he didn't particularly like her, but there was a pretty blonde who put up her long hair into a kind of doughnut with a black ribbon round it, whom he took to see films when the schoolboys and girls had a free Saturday afternoon. He had been driving tractors and other farm vehicles since he was nine years old, and as soon as he was eighteen he got a driver's licence and in the holidays, this last year of his school life, he took neighbours' daughters to dances and to the drive-in cinema that had just opened twenty kilometres from the farm. His sisters were married, by then; his parents often left him in charge of the farm over the weekend while they visited the young wives and grandchildren. When Thebedi saw the farmer and his wife drive away on a Saturday afternoon, the boot of their Mercedes filled with the fresh-killed poultry and vegetables from the garden that it was part of her father's work to tend, she knew that she must come not to the river-bed but up to the house. The house was an old one, thick-walled, dark against the heat. The kitchen was its lively thoroughfare, with servants, food supplies, begging cats and dogs, pots boiling over, washing being damped for ironing, and the big deep-freeze the missus had ordered from town, bearing a crocheted mat and vase of plastic irises. But the dining room with the bulging-legged heavy table was shut up in its rich, old smell of soup and tomato sauce. The sitting room curtains were drawn and the polished cabinet of the combination radio-record player silent. The door of the parents' bedroom was locked and the empty rooms where the girls had slept had sheets of plastic spread over the beds. It was in one of these that she and the farmer's son stayed together whole nights – almost: she had to get away before the house servants, who knew her, came in at dawn. There was a risk that someone would discover her or traces of her presence if he took her to his own bedroom, although she had looked into it many times when she was helping out in the house and knew well, there, the row of silver cups he had won at school.

When she was eighteen and the farmer's son nineteen and working with his father on the farm before entering a veterinary college, the boy Njabulo asked her father for her. The boy's parents met with hers and the money he was to pay in place of the cows it is customary to give a prospective bride's parents was settled upon. He had no cows to offer; he was a labourer on the Eysendyck farm, like her father. A bright youngster; old Eysendyck had taught him brick-laying and was using him for odd jobs in construction, around the place. She did not tell the farmer's son that her parents had arranged for her to marry. She did not tell him, either, before he left for his first term at the veterinary college, that she thought she was going to have a baby. Two months after her marriage to Njabulo, she gave birth to a daughter. There was no disgrace in that; among her people it is customary for a young man to make sure, before marriage, that the chosen girl is not barren, and Njabulo had made love to her then. But the infant was very light and did not quickly grow darker as most African babies do. Already at birth there was on its head a quantity of straight, fine floss, like that which carries the seeds of certain weeds in the veld. The unfocused eyes it opened were grey flecked with yellow. Njabulo was the matt, opaque coffee-grounds colour that has always been called black; the colour of Thebedi's legs on which beaded water looked oyster-shell blue, the same colour as Thebedi's face, where the black eyes, with their interested gaze and clear whites, were so dominant.

Njabulo made no complaint. Out of his farm labourer's earnings he bought from the Indian store a cellophane-windowed pack containing a pink plastic bath, six napkins, a card of safety pins, a knitted jacket, cap and bootees, a dress, and a tin of Johnson's Baby Powder, for Thebedi's baby.

When it was two weeks old Paulus Eysendyck arrived home from the veterinary college for the holidays. For the first time since he was a small boy he came right into the kraal. It was eleven o'clock in the morning. The men were at work in the lands. He looked about him, urgently; the women turned away, each not wanting to be the one approached to point out where Thebedi lived. Thebedi appeared, coming slowly from the hut that Njabulo had built in white man's style, with a tin chimney and a proper window with glass panes, set in as straight as walls made of unfired bricks would allow. She greeted him with hands brought together and a token movement representing the respectful bob with which she was accustomed to acknowledge she was in the presence of his father or mother. He lowered his head under the doorway of her home and went in. He said, 'I want to see. Show me.'

She had taken the bundle off her back before she came out into the light to face him. She moved between the iron bedstead made up with Njabulo's checked blankets and the small wooden table where the pink plastic bath stood among food and kitchen pots, and picked up the bundle from the snugly-blanketed grocer's box where it lay. The infant was asleep; she revealed the closed, pale, plump tiny face, with a bubble of spit at the corner of the mouth, the spidery pink hands stirring. She took off the woollen cap and the straight fine hair flew up after it in static electricity, showing gilded strands here and there. He said nothing. She was watching him as she had done when they were little, and the gang of children had trodden down a crop in their games or transgressed in some other way for which he, as the farmer's son, the white one among them, must intercede with the farmer. She disturbed the sleeping face by scratching or tickling gently at a cheek with one finger, and slowly the eyes opened, saw nothing, were still asleep, and then, awake, no longer narrowed, looked out at them, grey with yellowish flecks, his own hazel eyes.

He struggled for a moment with a grimace of tears, anger and self-pity. She could not put out her hand to him. He said, 'You haven't been near the house with it?'

She shook her head.

'Never?'

Again she shook her head.

'Don't take it out. Stay inside. Can't you take it away somewhere? You must give it to someone –'

She moved to the door with him.

He said, 'I'll see what I will do. I don't know.' And then he said: 'I feel like killing myself.'

Her eyes began to glow, to thicken with tears. For a moment there was the feeling between them that used to come when they were alone down at the river-bed.

He walked out.

Two days later, when his mother and father had left the farm for the day, he appeared again. The women were away on the lands, weeding, as they were employed to do as casual labour in summer; only the very old remained, propped up on the ground outside the huts in the flies and the sun. The child had not been well; it had diarrhoea. He asked her where its food was. She said, 'The milk comes from me.' He stood a moment and then went into Njabulo's house, where the child lay; she did not follow but stayed outside the door and watched without seeing an old crone who had lost her mind, talking to herself, talking to the fowls who ignored her.

She thought she heard small grunts from the hut, the kind of infant grunt that indicates stirring within a deep sleep. After a time, long or short she did not know, he came out and walked away with plodding stride (his father's gait) out of sight, towards his father's house.

The baby was not fed during the night and although she kept telling Njabulo it was sleeping, he saw for himself in the morning that it was dead. He comforted her with words and caresses. She did not cry but simply sat, staring at the door. Her hands were cold as dead chickens' feet to his touch.

Njabulo buried the little baby where farm workers were buried, in the place in the veld the farmer had given them. Some of the mounds had been left to weather away unmarked, others were covered with stones and a few had fallen wooden crosses. He was going to make a cross but before it was finished the police came and dug up the grave and took away the dead baby: someone – one of the other labourers? their women? – had reported that the baby that was almost white had died very soon after a visit by the farmer's son. Pathological tests on the infant corpse showed intestinal damage not always consistent with death by natural causes.

Thebedi went for the first time to the country town where Paulus had been to school, to give evidence at the preparatory examination into the charge of murder brought against him. She cried hysterically in the witness box, saying yes, yes (the gilt hoop earrings swung in her ears), she saw the accused pouring liquid into the baby's mouth. She said he had threatened to shoot her if she told anyone.

More than a year went by before, in that same town, the case was brought to trial. She came to Court with a new-born baby on her back. She wore gilt hoop earrings; she was calm; she said she had not seen what the white man did in the house.

Paulus Eysendyck said he had visited the hut but had not poisoned the child.

The Defence did not contest that there had been a love relationship between the accused and the girl, or that intercourse had taken place, but submitted there was no proof that the child was the accused's.

The judge told the accused there was a strong suspicion against him but not enough proof that he had committed the crime. The Court could not accept the girl's evidence because it was clear she had committed perjury either at this trial or at the preparatory examination. There was the suggestion in the mind of the Court that she might be an accomplice in the crime; but again, insufficient proof.

The judge commended the honourable behaviour of the husband (sitting in Court in a brown-and-yellow-quartered gold cap bought for Sundays) who had not rejected his wife and had 'even provided clothes for the unfortunate infant out of his slender means.'

The verdict on the accused was 'not guilty.'

The young white man refused to accept the congratulations of press and public and left the Court with his mother's raincoat shielding his face from photographers. His father said to the press, 'I will try and carry on as best I can to hold up my head in the district.'

Interviewed by the Sunday papers, who spelled her name in a variety of ways, the black girl, with photograph, was quoted: 'It was a thing of our childhood, we don't see each other any more.'

The Bamboo Blind

Seema Jena

It was late afternoon in October. Darkness had not crept in yet. She could still see some blue-grey patches through the window. An eerie dampness clung to the air after the shower of rain earlier on in the day as though it were complementing her state of mind. She tried hard, but eventually they came, tears. Wiping her face, Razia threw away the magazine she had been trying to read. She could not tear herself from the thoughts that had been nagging her the whole day. While anxiously awaiting Razak's return, she reproached herself for her behaviour towards her husband, but things were getting out of control and had to be dealt with decisively, she thought, defiance returning to her face.

From some corner of the house, voices could be heard sorting out the menu for the evening meal. 'One adds the *garam masala** last, you daughter of an owl!' her mother-in-law's voice boomed through the wall.

Thinking it was expected that she should offer some help, Razia tied her long disarrayed tresses into a knot and stepped out of her room, but realized that the family might feel awkward with her there. She switched on the television.

The news was relating the plight of the Kurds. Skipping through the channels to see if anything interesting was on, she realized that all the meaty bits were stacked away for the evening. Razak had once explained that such an arrangement suited people in

* *garam masala*: mixture of spices used for cooking

this country as they went out to work during the day, even the women. She envied their good fortune. Unlike her, they were not confined to four walls, where one day was little different from the next, like the daily tearing off a page from her wall calendar. However, none of the other residents ever seemed to be conscious of the monotony, not even the women. Her thoughts drifted towards a different scene in a far-off place, to the life behind the *chilman* (the bamboo blind), to the house where she had grown up, her father's.

Razia's father, Syed Mazhar Ali Shah, was regarded very highly among the leading citizens of the city. His family had lived in Lucknow for at least a hundred years. Now in his late sixties, Mazhar sahab had retired from the daily hassles of the tobacco business and had passed it on to the able hands of his four sons. Their house stood out from the rest of the houses in the street and apart from housing twenty-five humans of all shapes and sizes (excluding the servants of course), it was a monument to the tradition, culture and high values her ancestors represented. Razia had spent all her childhood and teens in this house. The façade had nothing to distinguish it from the other old houses of Lucknow. The front door opened on to the road, there was no compound wall, with just a few steps leading from the door to the street. What formed the most significant feature of the house was the massive inner courtyard which divided the house into two sections. There there were the ante-rooms, which housed the offices and provided space for the dozen employees, typists, accountants and the *babus**, where clients came to meet the younger Mazhars for business

---

*   *babus*: clerks

transactions and where they would sit talking, discussing, bargaining and hassling all day long.

Then there was the back section of the house which constituted the women's quarters. The front of this wing, opening to the courtyard, was covered by the *chilman*. Fifteen women of different ages, starting from the ten-month-old Farhana (Mazhar sahab's youngest granddaughter), to Amma (Mazhar sahab's mother), who was eighty-five, as well as all children under ten, inhabited this section of the house. The women, though hidden from the men behind this veil of thin bamboo strips held together with jute strings, scrutinized every movement that went on in the courtyard as well as kept a note of the people who visited the house. If at times, they felt that they had missed out on some juicy bits, they were extracted from the servants with great dexterity. However, the world behind the fifty-foot-long bamboo blind was very active, and each member of it was engaged in something throughout the day. Amma always had her pan[*] box open, making pans for the whole house. Begum Mazhar supervised the kitchen and the daily shopping list, allocating various chores to the servants. It was quite a job to be the unofficial head of such a large family.

Razia had loathed the whole arrangement behind the bamboo blind. 'That's a woman's life; our mothers had this life and so did their mothers,' Amma explained, moving the ground betel nut in her toothless mouth. 'Don't sin in this life, so you can face Him on the day of judgment,' she had said gravely. No one complained except her. Razia had completed her matriculation and with great difficulty persuaded the

---

[*]   pan: betel leaf

family to let her enrol in the local women's college. Suddenly, one day her scholastic career was terminated. A fellow student who also happened to be the daughter of her father's best friend eloped with a Christian boy she had met during an inter-college essay competition. The entire community was shocked. 'Ya Allah!' Begum Mazhar had exclaimed, raising her right hand to her forehead, 'that too, with an infidel! *Toba** *toba*! What is this world coming to? Tch . . . tch . . . tch.'

After the incident Razia was told by her brothers that she had acquired all the education that she would ever need and it would be worthwhile if she learned how to prepare *biryani** and learn *zardozi** embroidery from her sisters-in-law. 'These talents are far more valuable than any college degrees in a marriage,' said Rizvan, the eldest. She secretly wished that no one would ever come forward to marry her, but she knew that with her father's reputation and the dowry she would bring with her, many fathers looking for 'nice' girls had been encouraged to approach the mullah's* wife, who forwarded their applications to Begum Mazhar, with exceeding promptness.

One afternoon, a few months after the scandal of the elopement had died down, Nargis *khala** had rushed into the terrace, where Razia was drying her hair and announced breathlessly, 'I have got something here.' Her hand, hidden in her *dupatta**, shook. 'What would you give me if I show you this?' she said, taking out the hidden treasure, a coloured photograph of someone.

*   *toba*: an exclamation asking for God's forgiveness
     biryani: a dish of meat and rice
     zardozi: embroidery worked on a frame
     mullah: priest   *khala*: aunt   *dupatta*: long scarf

'This is the boy *bhai jaan*[*] has seen this morning.' Not again; must be some fat, ugly, stupid brat of some rich father, she thought. Her aunt went on with added gusto: 'He approves. The only thing he is worried about is that the boy lives in Vilayet and his family is there too.'

Razia pricked up her ears. 'Vilayet!'

She was no longer indifferent to the remaining bits of information pouring out of Nargis *khala*'s lips. Marrying someone living in England would be a dream come true. She glanced gingerly at the photograph left behind by her aunt. She studied the young face, the smart blue suit and the mischievous smile, the last observation making her blush. From that day on, she fasted and prayed that the alliance would come through. Her prayers were answered and a few days later the date of the wedding was fixed.

The *nikaah*[*] was a grand affair. Half the distinguished population of Lucknow turned up for the reception. After the wedding the couple went to Simla for a weekend. These were the most memorable days in Razia's life. Razak was very kind and considerate. He told her that his family lived together in Britain, that he had a large family and that she would not miss home and added, 'In many ways it is just like Lucknow.' She tried hard to hide the smile creeping up to her lips.

Razak's house in Manchester was not as palatial as her father's, but it sheltered fifteen people under its roof. Here, each family was allotted a room. Theirs was in a corner. For Razia the most attractive feature about the room was the window which overlooked the street that ran along the side of the house, although

[*]   *bhai jaan*: brother   *nikaah*: wedding ceremony

the view was not in any way spectacular. The street was lined with semi-detached houses like their own. The same people pursued the same activities day after day – children leaving and returning from school, the postman shoving mail twice a day through the flaps with his podgy fingers, people emptying their garbage into the bins. But the window was her sanctuary in a house where most of the people were still strangers.

She was ill at ease and uncomfortable with Razak's sisters, who spoke of sales, salons and the latest video releases, particularly the eldest one, Hasina, who always stared at Razia when they were together, minutely observing and judging her younger brother's wife.

After Razak had returned with her to Britain, he was busy with the new extension to the shop and had very little time to take her out. They had gone out only twice in all the months they had been in the country, once to visit some special relatives and family friends as was the custom for newly-weds. Razak stayed the whole day at the shop and in the evenings went out for a drink with a friend. Razia tried to picture what a pub looked like. Once when they were alone, she had broached the subject. He had replied matter-of-factly, 'Oh, it's just like a café where one orders things to eat and drink, lot of noise, smoke, nothing grand.' She wanted to ask if that was all then why go there every day, but checked herself, recollecting her grandmother's parting advice, 'Want to keep a man in your fist, never ask too many questions.'

Razak was in many ways easy to please; she forgot all her disappointments with his gentleness and love. His only plea to her was that he would not tolerate any complaints against his family. His mother was old, his sister had problems, his sister-in-law was illiterate, but she was different, she was educated, should she

stoop to their level? After that, Razia stopped
mentioning her daily discomforts to her husband,
until yesterday. She screwed up her nose as she
recollected yesterday's scene and the confrontation
she had with Razak's family.

Razia looked out of her window quite frequently
whenever she had nothing to do and Razak's sisters had
crowded into the living room. That her mother-in-law did
not approve of her standing near the window or sitting on
the sill was made clear by the arching of her eyebrows
whenever she caught Razia in the act, though she had
never verbally expressed her disapproval. The day before
when Hasina dropped in, Razia had greeted her and got
up to leave the room, mumbling some excuse.

'Do we stink?' Hasina's voice was sharp as a knife.
'Yes, tell me, do we stink? Or are we not good enough
for you, that you prefer the window gazing to us?'

In her confusion Razia could only mutter, 'But *baji*[*],
what harm is done to anybody if one looks out of a
window?'

'*Chup*; *badtameez*[*]! In your family do they talk back
to elders?' Hasina's voice had increased its volume to
such a degree that the children had left their games
and gathered in the living room to watch the game that
engaged the grown-ups. Razak's mother, feigning to be
deaf during this verbal exchange, suddenly shot a
warning look at her daughter, silencing her. Hurt and
humiliated, Razia ran out of the room with her
mother-in-law in tow.

Once in Razia's room the older lady started
speaking. '*Na*[*], *na*, *bete*[*], don't be upset with Hasina.

---

[*]   *baji*: respectful term for sister-in-law   *chup*: be quiet
      badtameez: ill-mannered   *na*: no   *bete*: child

She means well. What will people say if they always find you near the window?'

Razia could feel the tears trickling down her cheeks, she tried her best to suppress the sobs rising within her.

Her mother-in-law went on in the same sugary tone, 'You come from a decent family, do I have to tell you what is right and what is wrong . . .?' the old lady's voice trailed to a halt when she saw that Razia had started crying.

Her mother-in-law adopted a cajoling tone, 'Go to the shops tomorrow, one of the boys will take you, buy a sari . . . some bangles, *hain**. Now stop crying, Razak will be back soon; one shouldn't show a tearful face to a husband when he comes home, how would it make him feel? So unwelcome.' She patted Razia's back and left the room.

Razia decided to settle matters with her husband as soon as he got back. Once he was in, she banged the door and started the tirade of accusations: for always being partial to his family, her loneliness in a strange country, his lack of concern for her. She stumbled with the words, not knowing the right lines for the occasion, never having experienced the rage she felt at that moment. Razak could only stare at his wife, his mouth half-open, looking stupid and helpless. When he finally got the whole picture of the day's events he promised he would try to see a way out of her misery. She heard him trying to coax his mother, who sounded equally concerned by Hasina's behaviour. '*Allah mian**! Why don't you give me death instead of all this?' she exclaimed, the catch-phrase which put an end to all arguments in the house.

---

*   *hain*: okay?   *Allah mian*: Dear God!

Razia's thoughts were jostled by the familiar hoot of the car horn in the porch. He was late, trying to avoid her, she thought bitterly. She switched off the television. That morning, he had left hurriedly, not wanting another tearful scene with his wife. She had spent the whole day in her room, reading and watching television. She was looking forward to the evening and to seeing how Razak fulfilled his promise. 'Let's see how much of a man he is,' she kept telling herself.

Razak came in carrying a cardboard box. 'This is the answer to all your problems,' he said, looking fondly at her.

He summoned his eldest nephew to hold a chair for him on which he stood and screwed two thick nails into the frame of the window. He removed something long and noisy from the box and hung it from the nails and inspected it with a knowledgeable frown. The object was white and shiny, with thin strips held together with strings.

'This is known as a venetian blind. See, if you pull this string the strips flatten and if you pull the other string, the strips open up and you can see everything outside, even if the window is covered, come here and see for yourself.'

Dumb with disbelief at what she was being told, Razia got up from the chair, walked up to her husband and stood beside him. 'What?'

He turned to her, beaming like a knight in shining armour. 'Happy? See, I told you, I would do something.'

Razia was speechless for a few moments. Later when she was able to speak she said, 'In Lucknow, we call it the *chilman*.' She looked at his kind and earnest face and smiled. She did not wish to seem ungrateful.

Everyday Use

Alice Walker

I will wait for her in the yard that Maggie and I made so clean and wavy yesterday afternoon. A yard like this is more comfortable than most people know. It is not just a yard. It is like an extended living-room. When the hard clay is swept clean as a floor and the fine sand around the edges lined with tiny, irregular grooves, anyone can come and sit and look up into the elm tree and wait for the breezes that never come inside the house.

Maggie will be nervous until after her sister goes: she will stand hopelessly in corners, homely and ashamed of the burn scars down her arms and legs, eyeing her sister with a mixture of envy and awe. She thinks her sister has held life always in the palm of one hand, that 'no' is a word the world never learned to say to her.

You've no doubt seen those TV shows where the child who has 'made it' is confronted, as a surprise, by her own mother and father, tottering in weakly from backstage. (A pleasant surprise, of course: what would they do if parent and child came on the show only to curse out and insult each other?) On TV mother and child embrace and smile into each other's faces. Sometimes the mother and father weep, the child wraps them in her arms and leans across the table to tell how she would not have made it without their help. I have seen these programmes.

Sometimes I dream a dream in which Dee and I are suddenly brought together on a TV programme of this sort. Out of a dark and soft-seated limousine I am ushered into a bright room filled with many people. There I meet a smiling, grey, sporty man like Johnny Carson who shakes my hand and tells me what a fine girl I have. Then we are on the stage and Dee is embracing me with tears in her eyes. She pins on my dress a large orchid, even though she has told me once that she thinks orchids are tacky flowers.

In real life I am a large, big-boned woman with rough, man-working hands. In the winter I wear flannel night-gowns to bed and overalls during the day. I can kill and clean a hog as mercilessly as a man. My fat keeps me hot in zero weather. I can work outside all day, breaking ice to get water for washing; I can eat pork liver cooked over the open fire minutes after it comes steaming from the hog. One winter I knocked a bull calf straight in the brain between the eyes with a sledge hammer and had the meat hung up to chill before nightfall. But of course all this does not show on television. I am the way my daughter would want me to be: a hundred pounds lighter, my skin like an uncooked barley pancake. My hair glistens in the hot bright lights. Johnny Carson has much to do to keep up with my quick and witty tongue.

But that is a mistake. I know even before I wake up. Who even knew a Johnson with a quick tongue? Who can even imagine me looking a strange white man in the eye? It seems to me I have talked to them always with one foot raised in flight, with my head turned in whichever way is farthest from them. Dee, though. She would always look anyone in the eye. Hesitation was no part of her nature.

'How do I look, Mama?' Maggie says, showing just enough of her thin body enveloped in pink skirt and red blouse for me to know she's there, almost hidden by the door.

'Come out into the yard,' I say.

Have you ever seen a lame animal, perhaps a dog run over by some careless person rich enough to own a car, sidle up to someone who is ignorant enough to be kind to him? That is the way my Maggie walks. She has been like this, chin on chest, eyes on ground, feet in shuffle, ever since the fire that burned the other house to the ground.

Dee is lighter than Maggie, with nicer hair and a fuller figure. She's a woman now, though sometimes I forget. How long ago was it that the other house burned? Ten, twelve years? Sometimes I can still hear the flames and feel Maggie's arms sticking to me, her hair smoking and her dress falling off her in little black papery flakes. Her eyes seemed stretched open, blazed open by the flames reflected in them. And Dee. I see her standing off under the sweet gum tree she used to dig gum out of; a look of concentration on her face as she watched the last dingy grey board of the house fall in toward the red-hot brick chimney. Why don't you do a dance around the ashes? I'd wanted to ask her. She had hated the house that much.

I used to think she hated Maggie, too. But that was before we raised the money, the church and me, to send her to Augusta to school. She used to read to us without pity; forcing words, lies, other folks' habits, whole lives upon us two, sitting trapped and ignorant underneath her voice. She washed us in a river of make-believe, burned us with a lot of knowledge we didn't necessarily need to know. Pressed us to her with the serious way she read, to shove us away at just the moment, like dimwits, we seemed about to understand.

Dee wanted nice things. A yellow organdie dress to wear to her graduation from high school; black pumps to match a green suit she'd made from an old suit somebody gave me. She was determined to stare down any disaster in her efforts. Her eyelids would not flicker for minutes at a time. Often I fought off the temptation to shake her. At sixteen she had a style of her own: and knew what style was.

I never had an education myself. After second grade the school was closed down. Don't ask me why: in 1927 coloureds asked fewer questions than they do now. Sometimes Maggie reads to me. She stumbles along good-naturedly but can't see well. She knows she is not bright. Like good looks and money, quickness passed her by. She will marry John Thomas (who has mossy teeth in an earnest face) and then I'll be free to sit here and I guess just sing church songs to myself. Although I never was a good singer. Never could carry a tune. I was always better at a man's job. I used to love to milk till I was hooked in the side in '49. Cows are soothing and slow and don't bother you, unless you try to milk them the wrong way.

I have deliberately turned my back on the house. It is three rooms, just like the one that burned, except the roof is tin; they don't make shingle roofs any more. There are no real windows, just some holes cut in the sides, like the portholes in a ship, but not round and not square, with rawhide holding the shutters up on the outside. This house is in a pasture, too, like the other one. No doubt when Dee sees it she will want to tear it down. She wrote me once that no matter where we choose to live, she will manage to come see us. But she will never bring her friends. Maggie and I thought about this and Maggie asked me, 'Mama, when did Dee ever *have* any friends?'

She had a few. Furtive boys in pink shirts hanging about on washday after school. Nervous girls who never laughed. Impressed with her they worshipped the well-turned phrase, the cute shape, the scalding humour that erupted like bubbles in lye. She read to them.

When she was courting Jimmy T she didn't have much time to pay to us, but turned all her faultfinding power on him. He *flew* to marry a cheap city girl from a family of ignorant flashy people. She hardly had time to recompose herself.

When she comes I will meet – but there they are!

Maggie attempts to make a dash for the house, in her shuffling way, but I stay her with my hand. 'Come back here,' I say. And she stops and tries to dig a well in the sand with her toe.

It is hard to see them clearly through the strong sun. But even the first glimpse of leg out of the car tells me it is Dee. Her feet were always neat-looking, as if God himself had shaped them with a certain style. From the other side of the car comes a short, stocky man. Hair is all over his head a foot long and hanging from his chin like a kinky mule tail. I hear Maggie suck in her breath. 'Uhnnnh,' is what it sounds like. Like when you see the wriggling end of a snake just in front of your foot on the road. 'Uhnnnh.'

Dee next. A dress down to the ground, in this hot weather. A dress so loud it hurts my eyes. There are yellows and oranges enough to throw back the light of the sun. I feel my whole face warming from the heat waves it throws out. Earrings gold, too, and hanging down to her shoulders. Bracelets dangling and making

noises when she moves her arm up to shake the folds
of the dress out of her armpits. The dress is loose and
flows, and as she walks closer, I like it. I hear Maggie
go 'Uhnnnh' again. It is her sister's hair. It stands
straight up like the wool on a sheep. It is black as night
and around the edges are two long pigtails that rope
about like small lizards disappearing behind her ears.

'Wa-su-zo-Tean-o!' she says, coming on in that
gliding way the dress makes her move. The short
stocky fellow with the hair to his navel is all grinning
and he follows up with 'Asalamalakim, my mother and
sister!' He moves to hug Maggie but she falls back,
right up against the back of my chair. I feel her
trembling there and when I look up I see the
perspiration falling off her chin.

'Don't get up,' says Dee. Since I am stout it takes
something of a push. You can see me trying to move a
second or two before I make it. She turns, showing
white heels through her sandals, and goes back to the
car. Out she peeks next with a Polaroid. She stoops
down quickly and lines up picture after picture of me
sitting there in front of the house with Maggie
cowering behind me. She never takes a shot without
making sure the house is included. When a cow comes
nibbling around the edge of the yard she snaps it and
me and Maggie *and* the house. Then she puts the
Polaroid in the back seat of the car, and comes up and
kisses me on the forehead.

Meanwhile Asalamalakim is going through motions
with Maggie's hand. Maggie's hand is as limp as a fish,
and probably as cold, despite the sweat, and she keeps
trying to pull it back. It looks like Asalamalakim wants
to shake hands but wants to do it fancy. Or maybe he
don't know how people shake hands. Anyhow, he soon
gives up on Maggie.

'Well,' I say. 'Dee.'

'No, Mama,' she says. 'Not "Dee", Wangero Leewanika Kemanjo!'

'What happened to "Dee"?' I wanted to know.

'She's dead,' Wangero said. 'I couldn't bear it any longer, being named after the people who oppress me.'

'You know as well as me you was named after your aunt Dicie,' I said. Dicie is my sister. She named Dee. We called her 'Big Dee' after Dee was born.

'But who was *she* named after?' asked Wangero.

'Her mother,' I said, and saw Wangero was getting tired. 'That's about as far back as I can trace it,' I said. Though, in fact, I probably could have carried it back beyond the Civil War through the branches.

'Well,' said Asalamalakim, 'there you are.'

'Uhnnnh,' I heard Maggie say.

'There I was not,' I said, 'before "Dicie" cropped up in our family, so why should I try to trace it that far back?'

He just stood there grinning, looking down on me like somebody inspecting a Model A car. Every once in a while he and Wangero sent eye signals over my head.

'How do you pronounce this name?' I asked.

'You don't have to call me by it if you don't want to,' said Wangero.

'Why shouldn't I?' I asked. 'If that's what you want us to call you, we'll call you.'

'I know it might sound awkward at first,' said Wangero.

'I'll get used to it,' I said. 'Ream it out again.'

Well, soon we got the name out of the way. Asalamalakim had a name twice as long and three times as hard. After I tripped over it two or three times he told me to just call him Hakim-a-barber. I wanted to ask him was he a barber, but I didn't really think he was, so I didn't ask.

'You must belong to those beef-cattle peoples down the road,' I said. They said 'Asalamalakim' when they met you, too, but they didn't shake hands. Always too busy: feeding the cattle, fixing the fences, putting up salt-lick shelters, throwing down hay. When the white folks poisoned some of the herd the men stayed up all night with rifles in their hands. I walked a mile and a half just to see the sight.

Hakim-a-barber said, 'I accept some of their doctrines, but farming and raising cattle is not my style.' (They didn't tell me, and I didn't ask, whether Wangero (Dee) had really gone and married him.)

We sat down to eat and right away he said he didn't eat collards* and pork was unclean. Wangero, though, went on through the chitlins* and corn bread, the greens and everything else. She talked a blue streak over the sweet potatoes. Everything delighted her. Even the fact that we still used the benches her daddy made for the table when we couldn't afford to buy chairs.

'Oh, Mama!' she cried. Then turned to Hakim-a-barber. 'I never knew how lovely these benches are. You can feel the rump prints,' she said, running her hands underneath her and along the bench. Then she gave a sigh and her hand closed over Grandma Dee's butter dish. 'That's it!' she said. 'I knew there was something I wanted to ask you if I could have.' She jumped up from the table and went over in the corner where the churn stood, the milk in it clabber* by now. She looked at the churn and looked at it.

---

*   collards: kind of cabbage
     chitlins: small intestines of an animal, e.g. a pig
     clabber: curds, yoghurt

'This churn top is what I need,' she said. 'Didn't Uncle Buddy whittle it out of a tree you all used to have?'

'Yes,' I said.

'Uh huh,' she said happily. 'And I want the dasher, too.'

'Uncle Buddy whittle that, too?' asked the barber.

Dee (Wangero) looked up at me.

'Aunt Dee's first husband whittled the dash,' said Maggie so low you almost couldn't hear her. 'His name was Henry, but they called him Stash.'

'Maggie's brain is like an elephant's,' Wangero said, laughing. 'I can use the churn top as a centrepiece for the alcove table,' she said, sliding a plate over the churn, 'and I'll think of something artistic to do with the dasher.'

When she finished wrapping the dasher the handle stuck out. I took it for a moment in my hands. You didn't even have to look close to see where hands pushing the dasher up and down to make butter had left a kind of sink in the wood. In fact, there were a lot of small sinks; you could see where thumbs and fingers had sunk into the wood. It was beautiful light yellow wood, from a tree that grew in the yard where Big Dee and Stash had lived.

After dinner Dee (Wangero) went to the trunk at the foot of my bed and started rifling through it. Maggie hung back in the kitchen over the dishpan. Out came Wangero with two quilts. They had been pieced by Grandma Dee and then Big Dee and me had hung them on the quilt frames on the front porch and quilted them. One was in the Lone Star pattern. The other was Walk Around the Mountain. In both of them were scraps of dresses Grandma Dee had worn fifty and more years ago. Bits and pieces of Grandpa

Jarrell's Paisley shirts. And one teeny faded blue piece, about the size of a penny matchbox, that was from Great Grandpa Ezra's uniform that he wore in the Civil War.

'Mama,' Wangero said sweet as a bird. 'Can I have these old quilts?'

I heard something fall in the kitchen, and a minute later the kitchen door slammed.

'Why don't you take one or two of the others?' I asked. 'These old things was just done by me and Big Dee from some tops your grandma pieced before she died.'

'No,' said Wangero. 'I don't want those. They are stitched around the borders by machine.'

'That'll make them last better,' I said.

'That's not the point,' said Wangero. 'These are all pieces of dresses Grandma used to wear. She did all this stitching by hand. Imagine!' She held the quilts securely in her arms, stroking them.

'Some of the pieces, like those lavender ones, come from old clothes her mother handed down to her,' I said, moving up to touch the quilts. Dee (Wangero) moved back just enough so that I couldn't reach the quilts. They already belonged to her.

'Imagine!' she breathed again, clutching them closely to her bosom.

'The truth is,' I said, 'I promised to give them quilts to Maggie, for when she marries John Thomas.'

She gasped like a bee had stung her.

'Maggie can't appreciate these quilts!' she said. 'She'd probably be backward enough to put them to everyday use.'

'I reckon she would,' I said. 'God knows I been saving 'em for long enough with nobody using 'em. I hope she will!' I didn't want to bring up how I had offered Dee (Wangero) a quilt when she went away to college. Then she had told me they were old-fashioned, out of style.

'But they're *priceless*!' she was saying now, furiously; for she has a temper. 'Maggie would put them on the bed and in five years they'd be in rags. Less than that!'

'She can always make some more,' I said. 'Maggie knows how to quilt.'

Dee (Wangero) looked at me with hatred. 'You just will not understand. The point is these quilts, *these* quilts!'

'Well,' I said, stumped. 'What would *you* do with them?'

'Hang them,' she said. As if that was the only thing you *could* do with quilts.

Maggie by now was standing in the door. I could almost hear the sound her feet made as they scraped over each other.

'She can have them, Mama,' she said, like somebody used to never winning anything, or having anything reserved for her. 'I can 'member Grandma Dee without the quilts.'

I looked at her hard. She had filled her bottom lip with checkerberry snuff and it gave her face a kind of dopey, hangdog look. It was Grandma Dee and Big Dee who taught her how to quilt herself. She stood there with her scarred hands hidden in the folds of her skirt. She looked at her sister with something like fear but she wasn't mad at her. This was Maggie's portion. This was the way she knew God to work.

When I looked at her like that something hit me in the top of my head and ran down to the soles of my feet. Just like when I'm in church and the spirit of God touches me and I get happy and shout. I did something

I never had done before: hugged Maggie to me, then dragged her on into the room, snatched the quilts out of Miss Wangero's hands and dumped them into Maggie's lap. Maggie just sat there on my bed with her mouth open.

'Take one or two of the others,' I said to Dee.

But she turned without a word and went out to Hakim-a-barber.

'You just don't understand,' she said, as Maggie and I came out to the car.

'What don't I understand?' I wanted to know.

'Your heritage,' she said. And then she turned to Maggie, kissed her, and said, 'You ought to try to make something of yourself, too, Maggie. It's really a new day for us. But from the way you and Mama still live you'd never know it.'

She put on some sunglasses that hid everything above the tip of her nose and her chin.

Maggie smiled; maybe at the sunglasses. But a real smile, not scared. After we watched the car dust settle I asked Maggie to bring me a dip of snuff. And then the two of us sat there just enjoying, until it was time to go in the house and go to bed.

Lensey Namioka *emigrated with her family from China to the United States of America. In* The All-American Slurp *she gives examples of some of the difficulties she and her family experienced.*

Paul Bowles *was born in the United States of America. He first went to Morocco in 1931 and after the war decided to settle in Tangier, where he has lived for over half a century. Many of his stories, including* The Empty Amulet *are set in Morocco. As well as writing novels and short stories of his own, he has also translated the works of several Arabic authors into English, most notably the stories of Moroccan writer Mohammed Mrabet.*

In The Empty Amulet, *Habiba marries a man with modern ideas. Habiba does adapt to her changed lifestyle, but in a less positive and successful way than does Lensey Namioka.*

The All-American Slurp
Lensey Namioka

The first time our family was invited out to dinner in America, we disgraced ourselves while eating celery. We had emigrated to this country from China, and during our early days here we had a hard time with American table manners.

In China we never ate celery raw, or any other kind of vegetable raw. We always had to disinfect the vegetables in boiling water first. When we were presented with our first relish tray, the raw celery caught us unprepared.

We had been invited to dinner by our neighbours, the Gleasons. After arriving at the house, we shook hands with our hosts and packed ourselves into a sofa. As our family of four sat stiffly in a row, my younger brother and I stole glances at our parents for a clue as to what to do next.

Mrs Gleason offered the relish tray to Mother. The tray looked pretty, with its tiny red radishes, curly sticks of carrots, and long, slender stalks of pale green celery. 'Do try some of the celery, Mrs Lin,' she said. 'It's from a local farmer, and it's sweet.'

Mother picked up one of the green stalks, and Father followed suit. Then I picked up a stalk, and my brother did too. So there we sat, each with a stalk of celery in our right hand.

Mrs Gleason kept smiling. 'Would you like to try some of the dip, Mrs Lin? It's my own recipe: sour cream and onion flakes, with a dash of Tabasco sauce.'

Most Chinese don't care for dairy products, and in those days I wasn't even ready to drink fresh milk. Sour cream sounded perfectly revolting. Our family shook our heads in unison.

Mrs Gleason went off with the relish tray to the other guests, and we carefully watched to see what they did. Everyone seemed to eat the raw vegetable quite happily.

Mother took a bite of her celery. *Crunch*. 'It's not bad!' she whispered.

Father took a bite of his celery. *Crunch*. 'Yes, it *is* good,' he said, looking surprised.

I took a bite, and then my brother. *Crunch, crunch*. It was more than good; it was delicious. Raw celery has a slight sparkle, a zingy taste that you don't get in cooked celery. When Mrs Gleason came around with the relish tray, we each took another stalk of celery, except my brother. He took two.

There was only one problem: long strings ran through the length of the stalk, and they got caught in my teeth. When I help my mother in the kitchen, I always pull the strings out before slicing celery.

I pulled the strings out of my stalk. *Z-z-zip, z-z-zip*. My brother followed suit. *Z-z-zip, z-z-zip, z-z-zip*. To my left, my parents were taking care of their own stalks. *Z-z-zip, z-z-zip, z-z-zip*.

Suddenly I realized that there was dead silence except for our zipping. Looking up, I saw that the eyes of everyone in the room were on our family. Mr and Mrs Gleason, their daughter Meg, who was my friend, and their neighbours the Badels – they were all staring at us as we busily pulled the strings of our celery.

That wasn't the end of it. Mrs Gleason announced that dinner was served and invited us to the dining table. It was lavishly covered with platters of food, but we couldn't see any chairs around the table. So we helpfully carried over some dining chairs and sat down. All the other guests just stood there.

Mrs Gleason bent down and whispered to us, 'This is a buffet dinner. You help yourselves to some food and eat it in the living room.'

Our family beat a retreat back to the sofa as if chased by enemy soldiers. For the rest of the evening, too mortified to go back to the dining table, I nursed a bit of potato salad on my plate.

Next day Meg and I got on the school bus together. I wasn't sure how she would feel about me after the spectacle our family made at the party. But she was just the same as usual, and the only reference she made to the party was, 'Hope you and your folks got enough to eat last night. You certainly didn't take very much. Mom never tries to figure out how much food to prepare. She just puts everything on the table and hopes for the best.'

I began to relax. The Gleasons' dinner party wasn't so different from a Chinese meal after all. My mother also puts everything on the table and hopes for the best.

Meg was the first friend I had made after we came to America. I eventually got acquainted with a few other kids in school, but Meg was still the only friend I had.

My brother didn't have any problems making friends. He spent all his time with some boys who were teaching him baseball, and in no time he could speak English much faster than I could – not better, but faster.

I worried more about making mistakes, and I spoke carefully, making sure I could say everything right before opening my mouth. At least I had a better accent than my parents, who never really got rid of their Chinese accent, even years later. My parents had both studied English in school before coming to America, but what they had studied was mostly written English, not spoken.

Father's approach to English was a scientific one. Since Chinese verbs have no tense, he was fascinated by the way English verbs changed form according to whether they were in the present, past imperfect, perfect, pluperfect, future or future perfect tense. He was always making diagrams of verbs and their inflexions, and he looked for opportunities to show off his mastery of the pluperfect and future perfect tenses, his two favourites. 'I shall have finished my project by Monday,' he would say smugly.

Mother's approach was to memorize lists of polite phrases that would cover all possible social situations. She was constantly muttering things like 'I'm fine, thank you. And you?' Once she accidentally stepped on someone's foot, and hurriedly blurted, 'Oh, that's quite all right!' Embarrassed by her slip, she resolved to do better next time. So when someone stepped on *her* foot, she cried, 'You're welcome!'

In our own different ways, we made progress in learning English. But I had another worry, and that was my appearance. My brother didn't have to worry, since Mother bought him blue jeans for school, and he dressed like all the other boys. But she insisted that girls had to wear skirts. By the time she saw that Meg and the other girls were wearing jeans, it was too late. My school clothes were bought already, and we didn't have money left to buy new outfits for me. We had too many other things to buy first, like furniture, pots, and pans.

The first time I visited Meg's house, she took me upstairs to her room, and I wound up trying on her clothes. We were pretty much the same size, since Meg was shorter and thinner than average. Maybe that's how we became friends in the first place. Wearing Meg's jeans and T-shirt, I looked at myself in the mirror. I could almost pass for an American – from the back anyway. At least the kids in school wouldn't stop and stare at me in the hallways, which was what they did when they saw me in my white blouse and navy blue skirt that went a couple of inches below the knees.

When Meg came to my house, I invited her to try on my Chinese dresses, the ones with a high collar and slits up the sides. Meg's eyes were bright as she looked at herself in the mirror. She struck several sultry poses, and we nearly fell over laughing.

The dinner party at the Gleasons' didn't stop my growing friendship with Meg. Things were getting better for me in other ways too. Mother finally bought me some jeans at the end of the month, when Father got his pay cheque. She wasn't in any hurry about buying them at first, until I worked on her. This is what I did. Since we didn't have a car in those days, I often ran down to the neighbourhood store to pick up things for her. The groceries cost less at a big supermarket, but the closest one was many blocks away. One day, when she ran out of flour, I offered to borrow a bike from our neighbour's son and buy a ten-pound bag of flour at the big supermarket. I mounted the boy's bike and waved to Mother. 'I'll be back in five minutes!'

Before I started pedalling, I heard her voice behind me. 'You can't go out in public like that! People can see all the way up to your thighs!'

'I'm sorry,' I said innocently. 'I thought you were in a hurry to get the flour.' For dinner we were going to have pot-stickers (fried Chinese dumplings), and we needed a lot of flour.

'Couldn't you borrow a girl's bicycle?' complained Mother. 'That way your skirt won't be pushed up.'

'There aren't too many of those around,' I said. 'Almost all the girls wear jeans while riding a bike, so they don't see any point buying a girl's bike.'

We didn't eat pot-stickers that evening, and Mother was thoughtful. Next day we took the bus downtown and she bought me a pair of jeans. In the same week, my brother made the baseball team of his junior high school, Father started taking driving lessons, and Mother discovered rummage sales. We soon got all the furniture we needed, plus a dart board and a 1,000-piece jigsaw puzzle (fourteen hours later, we discovered that it was a 999-piece jigsaw puzzle).

There was hope that the Lins might become a normal American family after all.

Then came our dinner at the Lakeview restaurant.

The Lakeview was an expensive restaurant, one of those places where a headwaiter dressed in tails conducted you to your seat, and the only light came from candles and flaming desserts. In one corner of the room a lady harpist played tinkling melodies.

Father wanted to celebrate, because he had just been promoted. He worked for an electronics company, and after his English started improving, his superiors decided to appoint him to a position more suited to his training. The promotion not only brought a higher salary but was also a tremendous boost to his pride.

Up to then we had eaten only in Chinese restaurants. Although my brother and I were becoming fond of hamburgers, my parents didn't care much for western food, except chow mein.

But this was a special occasion, and Father asked his co-workers to recommend a really elegant restaurant. So there we were at the Lakeview, stumbling after the headwaiter in the murky dining room.

At our table we were handed our menus, and they were so big that to read mine I almost had to stand up again. But why bother? It was mostly in French, anyway.

Father, being an engineer, was always systematic. He took out a pocket French dictionary. 'They told me that most of the items would be in French, so I came prepared.' He even had a pocket flashlight, the size of a marking pen. While Mother held the flashlight over the menu, he looked up the items that were in French.

'*Pâté en croûte,*' he muttered. 'Let's see . . . *pâté* is paste . . . *croûte* is crust . . . hmm . . . a paste in crust.'

The waiter stood looking patient. I squirmed and died at least fifty times.

At long last Father gave up. 'Why don't we just order four complete dinners at random?' he suggested.

'Isn't that risky?' asked Mother. 'The French eat some rather peculiar things, I've heard.'

'A Chinese can eat anything a Frenchman can eat,' Father declared.

The soup arrived in a plate. How do you get soup up from a plate? I glanced at the other diners, but the ones at the nearby tables were not on their soup course, while the more distant ones were invisible in the darkness.

Fortunately my parents had studied books on western etiquette before they came to America. 'Tilt your plate,' whispered my mother. 'It's easier to spoon the soup up that way.'

She was right. Tilting the plate did the trick. But the etiquette book didn't say anything about what you did after the soup reached your lips. As any respectable Chinese knows, the correct way to eat your soup is to slurp. This helps to cool the liquid and prevent you from burning your lips. It also shows your appreciation.

We showed our appreciation. *Shloop*, went my father. *Shloop*, went my mother. *Shloop, shloop*, went my brother, who was the hungriest.

The lady harpist stopped playing to take a rest. And in the silence, our family's consumption of soup suddenly seemed unnaturally loud. You know how it sounds on a rocky beach when the tide goes out and the water drains from all those little pools? They go *shloop, shloop, shloop*. That was the Lin family, eating soup.

At the next table a waiter was pouring wine. When a large *shloop* reached him, he froze. The bottle continued to pour, and red wine flooded the tabletop and into the lap of a customer. Even the customer didn't notice anything at first, being also hypnotized by the *shloop, shloop, shloop*.

It was too much. 'I need to go to the toilet,' I mumbled, jumping to my feet. A waiter, sensing my urgency, quickly directed me to the ladies' room.

I splashed cold water on my burning face and, as I dried myself with a paper towel, I stared into the mirror. In this perfumed ladies' room, with its pink-and-silver wallpaper and marbled sinks, I looked completely out of place. What was I doing here? What was our family doing in the Lakeview restaurant? In America?

The door to the ladies' room opened. A woman came in and glanced curiously at me. I retreated into one of the toilet cubicles and latched the door.

Time passed – maybe half an hour, maybe an hour. Then I heard the door open again, and my mother's voice. 'Are you in there? You're not sick, are you?'

There was real concern in her voice. A girl can't leave her family just because they slurp their soup. Besides, the toilet cubicle had a few drawbacks as a permanent residence. 'I'm all right,' I said, undoing the latch.

Mother didn't tell me how the rest of the dinner went, and I didn't want to know. In the weeks following, I managed to push the whole thing into the back of my mind, where it jumped out at me only a few times a day. Even now, I turn hot all over when I think of the Lakeview restaurant.

But by the time we had been in this country for three months, our family was definitely making progress toward becoming Americanized. I remember my parents' first PTA meeting. Father wore a neat suit and tie, and Mother put on her first pair of high heels. She stumbled only once. They met my homeroom teacher and beamed as she told them that I would make honour roll soon at the rate I was going. Of course Chinese etiquette forced Father to say that I was a very stupid girl and Mother to protest that the teacher was showing favouritism toward me. But I could tell they were both very proud.

The day came when my parents announced that they wanted to give a dinner party. We had invited Chinese friends to eat with us before, but this dinner was going to be different. In addition to a Chinese-American family, we were going to invite the Gleasons.

'Gee, I can hardly wait to have dinner at your house,' Meg said to me. 'I just *love* Chinese food.'

That was a relief. Mother was a good cook, but I wasn't sure if people who ate sour cream would also eat chicken gizzards stewed in soy sauce.

Mother decided not to take a chance with chicken gizzards. Since we had western guests, she set the table with large dinner plates, which we never used in Chinese meals. In fact we didn't use individual plates at all, but picked up food from the platters in the middle of the table and brought it directly to our rice bowls. Following the practice of Chinese-American restaurants, Mother also placed large serving spoons on the platters.

The dinner started well. Mrs Gleason exclaimed at the beautifully arranged dishes of food: the colourful candied fruit in the sweet-and-sour pork dish, the noodle-thin shreds of chicken meat stir-fried with tiny peas, and the glistening pink prawns in a ginger sauce.

At first I was too busy enjoying my food to notice how the guests were doing. But soon I remembered my duties. Sometimes guests were too polite to help themselves and you had to serve them with more food.

I glanced at Meg, to see if she needed more food, and my eyes nearly popped out at the sight of her plate. It was piled with food: the sweet-and-sour meat pushed right against the chicken shreds, and the chicken sauce ran into the prawns. She had been taking food from a second dish before she finished eating her helping from the first!

Horrified, I turned to look at Mrs Gleason. She was dumping rice out of her bowl and putting it on her dinner plate. Then she ladled prawns and gravy on top of the rice and mixed everything together, the way you mix sand, gravel and cement to make concrete.

I couldn't bear to look any longer, and I turned to Mr Gleason. He was chasing a pea around his plate. Several times he got it to the edge, but when he tried to pick it up with his chopsticks, it rolled back toward the centre of the plate again. Finally he put down his chopsticks and picked up the pea with his fingers. He really did! A grown man!

All of us, our family and the Chinese guests, stopped eating to watch the activities of the Gleasons. I wanted to giggle. Then I caught my mother's eyes on me. She frowned and shook her head slightly, and I understood the message: the Gleasons were not used to Chinese ways, and they were just coping the best they could. For some reason I thought of celery strings.

When the main courses were finished, Mother brought out a platter of fruit. 'I hope you weren't expecting a sweet dessert,' she said. 'Since the Chinese don't eat dessert, I didn't think to prepare any.'

'Oh, I couldn't possibly eat dessert!' cried Mrs Gleason. 'I'm simply stuffed!'

Meg had different ideas. When the table was cleared, she announced that she and I were going for a walk. 'I don't know about you, but I feel like dessert,' she told me, when we were outside. 'Come on, there's a Dairy Queen down the street. I could use a big chocolate milkshake!'

Although I didn't really want anything more to eat, I insisted on paying for the milkshakes. After all, I was still hostess.

Meg got her large chocolate milkshake and I had a small one. Even so, she was finishing hers while I was only half done. Toward the end she pulled hard on her straws and went *shloop, shloop*.

'Do you always slurp when you eat a milkshake?' I asked, before I could stop myself.

Meg grinned. 'Sure. All Americans slurp.'

The Empty Amulet[*]
Paul Bowles

Habiba's father, who was the concierge[*] at the principal hotel of the city, provided a comfortable life for his family, but he was unusually strict. Some of Habiba's friends among girls of her age had been to school and even passed their examinations, so that they could become secretaries and bookkeepers and dentists' assistants. Habiba's father, however, considered all this highly immoral, and would not hear of allowing her to attend school. Instead, she learned embroidery and knitting, which she accomplished using modern German machines he bought for her.

When Moumen, a young man of the neighbourhood, came to ask for Habiba's hand in marriage, her father accepted because he knew that the young man worked at a nearby hospital as an intern, and thus had permanent employment. Habiba was not consulted. She was delighted to escape from the parental home and the everlasting embroidery.

Since Moumen was a young man with modern ideas, he did not lock his bride into the house when he went out to work. On the contrary, he urged her to get to know the young married women of the quarter. Soon, she was part of a group whose members met each day, first at one house and then another.

Habiba was not long in discovering that the principal topic of conversation amongst these ladies was the state of their health. Every one of them

<hr>

[*] amulet: trinket worn as a protection against evil
concierge: caretaker

claimed to suffer from some affliction or indisposition. This discountenanced Habiba, for, always having been in the best of health, she could only sit and listen when the subject of ailments arose.

One day she awoke with a headache. When her friends arrived that morning to see her, she complained of the pain. Immediately she was the centre of attention. The following day when they inquired about her health, she told them she still had the pain in her head. And indeed, as she thought about it, it seemed to her that she could feel an occasional throb. Each woman was ready with a different remedy, but they all agreed that a visit to the tomb of Sidi Larbi would provide the surest relief.

There were three other women in the group who were eager to make the pilgrimage. Accordingly, a few days later Habiba went off with them in a large taxi to Sidi Larbi. They took along a picnic lunch, which Habiba, following their advice, washed down with a glass of water containing a large pinch of black earth from outside the mausoleum. Each of them gathered a pile of this dirt to take home for future use. At the end of the day in the open air, Habiba was unable to feel even a trace of headache. Drink the dirt five nights in a row, they told her.

When she got home she hid the packet of earth, knowing that Moumen disapproved of Moroccan medicine. His objections to it were so vehement that she suspected him of being afraid of it, in the same way that she was frightened of entering the hospital where he worked. The nauseating medicinal odours, the bins of bloody bandages, the shining syringes, all filled her with dread.

Scarcely a week passed that some of the young women among her friends did not make a pilgrimage to the tomb of Sidi Hussein or Sidi Larbi or some other not too distant shrine. It seemed to Moumen that Habiba was always on the verge of visiting one saint or another; either she had pains in her back, or cramps, or a stiff neck. Whatever trouble she named, there was always a saint who could cure it.

One evening Moumen went unexpectedly into the kitchen and found Habiba stirring some earth into a glass of water.

Habiba! You can't do that! he cried. It's what they did a hundred years ago.

And two hundred and five hundred, she retorted, her eyes on the glass.

You're a savage! It makes me sick to look at you!

Habiba was unperturbed. She knew he considered the pills and injections used by the Nazarenes superior to the *baraka** of the saints. This had nothing to do with her, she decided; she was not going to be influenced by him.

I have pains in my side, she said. Rahma had the same pains, and the mud from Sidi Yamani got rid of them in twenty-four hours.

If you'll come to the hospital tomorrow morning, I'll give you some pills, he told her, intending, if she agreed, to hand her some sugar-coated pills containing nothing at all, since he knew her to be in perfect health.

This is my medicine, she said, moving the glass in a circular fashion, to dissolve all the mud.

It cost him an effort not to wrest the glass away from her and dash it to the floor. He shook his head. A beautiful girl like you swallowing dirt!

Habiba leaned back against the sink and calmly drank the contents of the glass.

---

* *baraka*: beneficent psychic power contained in an amulet

The day Moumen learned that Habiba was carrying a child, he sat for a long time in a café, trying to think of a way to keep her from going on any more of her absurd pilgrimages. At one point he looked up and noticed a book of cigarette papers that someone had left on the table next to him. He reached over for it. Idly he pulled out two of the little sheets of rice-paper and crumpled them between his fingers. As he glanced down at the tiny ball of paper, the idea came to him.

He paid the *qahouaji**, and taking the book of cigarette papers with him, he made his way down into the *Medina** to see a friend who worked as a goldsmith. He wanted him to make a tiny gold cage just big enough to hold a baraka. While they were discussing the size and price of the piece of jewellery, Moumen surreptitiously reached into his pocket and pulled out two cigarette papers, which he rolled into a ball. When they had come to an agreement, he asked the goldsmith for a bit of silk thread, and wound a short length of it around the ball of paper.

Here's the baraka, he told the man, who dropped it into an envelope on which Moumen wrote his name, and promised to have the chain and pendant ready the following afternoon.

The small gold cage on its slender chain made a pretty necklace. When he took it home and fastened it around Habiba's neck, he told her: This baraka is from a very great *fqih**. It's to protect the baby.

He was a bit ashamed, but greatly relieved, to see how much the gift meant to her. During the months that followed, when she might have been expected to

* *qahouaji*: proprietor *Medina*: ancient part of a city
fqih: a man supposedly versed in the Koran, often consulted as an exorcist

suffer discomfort, she was uncomplaining and happy. She told her friends that her husband did not want her to ride in taxis on country roads because it might be bad for the baby, and they nodded their heads sagely. Besides, said Habiba, I don't need to go any more.

Hamdoul'lah[*], they said.

The baby was born: a robust little creature who passed through his infancy unscathed by illness. Habiba herself was radiantly healthy; since the day she had begun to wear the cage over her heart she had not once complained of a symptom. It was the possession she valued above all others. The days of making pilgrimages and swallowing mud were far behind; Moumen was pleased with himself for having found such a simple solution to a difficult problem.

One summer afternoon when Habiba rose from her siesta, she took the necklace from the table to fasten it around her neck, for she did not like to be without it. For some reason the chain snapped, and the cage slid to the floor, where it rolled out of sight. As she moved around the room looking for it, she felt a light crunch beneath her foot, and realized that she had stepped on it. The lid had broken off and the ball of paper had tumbled out. She gathered up the broken cage and the baraka that had been inside. The silk thread slipped off and the cigarette papers sprang open.

Habiba uncreased both. Nothing was written on either paper. She held them up to the light and saw the watermarks; then she understood what they were. She sat perfectly still for a long time, while her sense of injury was slowly replaced by fury with Moumen for having deceived her, and for so long a period of time. When Moumen got home that evening and saw her

* *Hamdoul'lah*: Thanks to God

face, he knew that the hour of reckoning had come. Habiba shouted at him, she wept, she sulked, she said she would never believe him again as long as she lived.

For several days she would not speak to Moumen; when finally one morning she did, it was to announce that she felt dizzy and had pains in her stomach. To his dismay he saw that for the first time she did look ill.

Thanks to your lies I went all that time without any baraka, she said bitterly.

Yes, but you were well all that time, he reminded her.

And that's why I'm sick now! she screamed. It's your fault!

Moumen did not attempt to answer her; he had learned the futility of expecting her to follow a logical train of thought.

Before the week was out, Habiba was on her way to Sidi Larbi with two of her friends. From that time onward Moumen heard nothing from her but an unvarying stream of complaints, cut short only on the day they were divorced.

Facing the Future

Claire Macquet *was born in South Africa in 1941, into a rural white working-class family. She left the country in the mid-1960's shortly after the imprisonment of leaders of the African National Congress.*

Doris Lessing *was born of British parents in Persia in 1919. At the age of five she was taken to Southern Rhodesia (now Zimbabwe), where she spent her childhood growing up on a large farm.*

Both writers have in common a hatred of the racially divisive policies of the governments of their countries. They also grew up in rural areas very similar to those in the following stories. Both Hennie in Mondi *and the boy in A Sunrise on the Veld are faced with questions and uncertainties about life. They also make some decisions.*

Mondi

Claire Macquet

In the middle of nowhere, the school bus screeched to a halt. A rather scruffy, mouse-haired girl tumbled out. She shook herself straight, shuffling in boots that seemed to be made of lead.

'Satchel!' she shouted.

An arm reached out through the window and tossed a hide bag with a big iron buckle.

'Ta.' She hauled the bag on to her shoulder, and lifted a khaki beret.

'Make speed Hennie,' somebody yelled from the bus in his rumbling Afrikaans language. 'There's gonna be a donder-'n-blitzen of a storm.*'

* donder-'n-blitzen of a storm: a violent thunderstorm

That was no lie. Hennie lifted her head and smelt the thick wetness of the wind. The gold had gone out in her father's maizefields and the sky was shutting down against the mountains. Soon lightning would crack itself against the peaks and then a wave of wind and hail and water would wash out the world. 'Ja*, Ja,' she called back gaily, and waved until the bus lurched off.

She walked, not, as one would expect, up the track to the van Rensberg farm, but across the veld to a clump of thorn trees. The storm would break in at best half an hour, but Hennie was not afraid.

Mondi and the pony would be waiting for her beneath the trees. Mondi had no fear of storms and, nor, when she was with Mondi, had the pony – called Intusi because her forehead blaze was white as milk. Maybe they would race to beat the storm; maybe they would huddle it out; maybe they would just charge through it. Mondi would know which. Though not afraid, Hennie was a little excited, partly by the sudden cooling and the wind running waves through the grass, but mainly because the best moment of all the day was coming soon. She would pull off her boot and caliper* and Mondi would help her on to Intusi's bare back. Then her poor, soft, unmade foot would curl back into its mouse-shape and be comfortable; then, doubled up with Mondi on Intusi, she could outrun any girl anywhere.

Hennie was the only child of Martinus van Rensberg, whose family had farmed here in Natal, in the stony foothills of the Drakensberg Mountains, for more than a hundred years. They, the van Rensbergs – shoulder to shoulder with the giants – the Pretoriuses, the

---

* Ja: yes   caliper: a corrective metal splint for the leg

Retiefs, the Maritzes – had fulfilled the Bible's prophecy and taken this land from the Zulus by force of arms. Their triumph, though, was short, for the Queen of England had sent regiments of redcoats and traitorous African clans against them and they, like the Zulus, were defeated. But not totally and not for ever: they had kept their language, religion and, what really mattered, the land. And now, in the 1950s, they were running the government. The Bible had not been wrong. But, typical of this false world, they had no money; the rednecks in their posh cities kept that for themselves.

Hennie's father, in his rare light moments, liked to stand on the stoep[*], legs splayed, with his pipe and his brandy, chatting to the oldest of his farmhands about these things. They, learning on their knobkerries[*] in the yard, and smoking pipes of even stronger tobacco, remembered their own stories of the Boers[*] pouring down the mountains with their covered wagons and herds of skinny cattle. Those herds had been much improved when the Zulus' cattle was added to them.

'You see, *Bomadala*[*],' Hennie's father would say, 'we brought you law and civilization. We stopped you killing each other. Now you can all have thirty cows and buy yourselves nice fat wives, heh!'

And the old men would chuckle and wait until the baas[*] had had enough brandy to be in the mood to bring out a jug of the fiery stuff for them to pass around. They always changed the subject if he started talking about the future, because then his jovial mood – and with it the promise of brandy – would vanish.

[*] stoep: verandah   knobkerries: round-headed sticks
Boer: South African of Dutch descent
Bomadala: old men   baas: master

The baas had a big strong wife who could make wonderful mealiebread and *vetkoek*; but she, who should have borne seven sons, had given him only this one half-child, a girl who would not grow straight enough to get herself a man who had served in the army and could run the farm. They knew that the baas tried hard not to notice that she was only a girl. Perhaps, even, because she was not a proper girl, he could pretend she was a boy and would be able to do man's work, run the farm: she, who would never wield a sjambok*, whom nobody would bother to obey, who could not even do women's work like hoeing and weeding; a soft girl who took no pleasure in hunting even though she could ride a horse pretty well. They thought of their own sons and grandsons powerful as mules and working in the gold mines, and they pitied the baas with all their hearts.

Martinus van Rensberg never spoke to the old men about his family. He spoke about the government's promise to give more help to farmers. He spoke about the new education system which would close down the poverty-stricken mission schools and give the Bomadala's grandchildren teaching in useful things like cattle-dipping and bantu* crafts. He spoke about the black men in Pietermaritzburg who wore spats and waistcoats and pretended to read newspapers, and the old men agreed that this was shocking.

Nonetheless, they knew all about the troubles of the van Rensburg family. They knew that the missus was waiting for her maiden auntie to die to get a hundred pounds for an operation on Hennie's club foot. They knew that the baas owed the government more money than his farm was worth. They knew that the brandy

* sjambok: a whip   bantu: African

they would be drinking was cheap rough stuff, a white man's drink, but only just.

Mondi, as usual, was sitting under the tree writing in the dust with her long fingers. The pony, untethered, was munching grass a few feet away. Hennie looked at Mondi's thin black shoulders, hunched over the work, her legs, stretched out before her, ending in two perfectly-made dust-stained feet. She went up close; she read the English words: 'I go. I went. I will go. I have gone. I had gone. I was going. I will have gone.'

'When do you say "I gone", Hennitjie?,' said Mondi without looking up.

'When you've finished going, I guess,' said Hennie uncertainly. 'I dunno. I hate English. It's a stupid language. I dunno why they have to make up such complicated ways of saying things instead of saying them straight.'

As if in agreement, a long, low growl of thunder rolled down from the mountains. Before the pony had even lifted its head to whinny, Mondi was on her feet and, catching the dangling reins, had led it under the bushes.

'Shush-shu-shu,' she told Intusi, 'the lightning's still miles away.'

Hennie watched with pleasure, knowing that soon she would be on the pony's back, clinging to her mane, Mondi's powerful knees holding them firm against the rocking canter, the rush of wind, the rain throwing itself at them. But first there was an important ritual. She tossed the satchel to Mondi. 'Have a look.'

Mondi undid the big iron buckle with care and drew out two, three dog-eared books. Her brow, almost always serious, was furrowed. '*A Christmas Carol* by

Charles Dickens': she pronounced the words carefully.
After wiping her hands a second time on her pants, she
opened the pages and stared at the small, dense print.
'Man, this is real English, Hennitjie,' she said.

'Ja man. We started it this week. It's hellava hard.
It's called a novel.'

'It's got two names?'

'No man, a novel means a story, a long one that's
really hard. D'ya wanna try it? That, there at the
bottom, that's a dictionary, a proper one.'

Mondi shook her head. 'If it's hard for you, it's not
good for me. I'll stick with your geography book, and
your biology – that's the best one. I've been trying to
remember since yesterday which one of a snake's
lungs is the big one. Can I look?'

Hennie nodded tersely. She sat down to wait while
Mondi peered at the pages, and began to unbuckle her
boots.

Hennie was nearly thirteen, two or perhaps three
years Mondi's junior, and any stupid could see that she
was beginning to outstrip Mondi in learning. The
shame of this was that to Mondi learning mattered so
much. It was one of those dumb things because Mondi
couldn't do anything with learning even if she got it.
She would never get a pass[*] to look for a reading-
and-writing job in town; she was too useful on the farm
where she belonged. And the new government had
promised to do much more to help farmers keep their
good labour. Mondi knew all that; there was no point
in telling her. And what was dumber than dumb was
that learning didn't matter to anybody else, certainly
not to Hennie's father, who seemed almost ashamed

[*]   pass: a document permitting black people to work at a job
       outside the area to which they had been assigned

that she did fairly well at school – it reminded him that she was a girl. In Mondi's studies Mr van Rensberg took a slight interest, once giving Mondi sixpence when she moved up a grade.

Mondi had started working for the van Rensbergs when she was about six. Because she was lanky and tended to drop things, she was used out in the kitchen garden and didn't ordinarily come to the house. It was chance that brought the girls together. Hennie's mother had seen Mondi among the cabbages, making little clay cattle that seemed almost alive. So she had brought her into the yard to amuse her whimpering child, and she rewarded her services with a koeksister* every Saturday. Hennie whined much less after that and even seemed to grow a little. Mondi too had gained – and more than cookies – for, at about the age of nine, she was taken on to clean the stables. And there she showed such a knack with horses that she was allowed time off on Mondays and Thursdays to attend the afternoon shifts at the mission school a few miles away. She was allowed to ride the pony to school in exchange for collecting Hennie from the school bus afterwards. Mondi, Mr van Rensberg said, sometimes a little resentfully, was the most privileged girl on the farm. Then Mondi, who had been stony-faced even as a little child, put on the deep frown which turned her old well beyond her years, but said nothing in reply.

Mondi, Hennie and Intusi often roamed on the way home. Hennie, wanting the rides to go on forever, delayed the end by any means possible. They had ridden through many summer storms before. They had been all over the farm and beyond – down to the river, up

* koeksister: biscuit

to the waterfall at the foot of the mountains, and to Mondi's home, a little cluster of round mud huts, thatched, and painted with lime and red clay slip. There they had watched Mondi's little brothers and sisters making clay figures (not cattle, but guns and tanks). Mondi's mother worked till late and had no money for a kerosene lamp, so sometimes on the dark winter evenings the two girls had seized their chance and drunk the sour kaffir beer* until they were awash with giggles and Intusi had to find the way back to the farmhouse.

But they had never been to the mission together. Hennie was frightened of nuns, these foreign white women who moved about like boats in their funny clothes, and ate Jesus, and lived with blacks, and caused trouble on the farms. She knew that Mondi thought the world of them, so she kept this to herself. But she also knew that the mission school had hardly any exercise-books or pencils, so she shared hers with Mondi – as far as she could without being caught.

Mondi looked up from the book. 'Frogs and snakes grow lungs; that's easy, but English really is hard, isn't it, Hennitjie,' she said.

'Ja. And English people, you know, they talk ever so fast and clippy, like birds, like they were chewing tobacco really fast. I've seen them, you know, the doctors at the hospital in Pietermaritzburg talking about my foot. Hellava stupid.'

'I guess.' Mondi had never been to Underberg, let alone Pietermaritzburg, but she had heard the nuns speaking French among themselves – sweet pure voices rising and twining like birdsong – and now that she had entered the third grade, English classes had

---

*   kaffir beer: native beer usually made from maize or millet

begun. These were solemn tones, full of power: 'I go; I will go; I went,' and, her mouth watering with the tension of separating out the breathy sounds, the magnificent 'I will have gone.' Mondi could speak and write Zulu, Xhosa and Afrikaans and sing (without understanding a word) the whole of the Latin Mass. To her there was nothing especially strange about people talking like birds chewing tobacco; the Tower of Babel was completely natural – cows talked a different language from goats – the world was not made to fit just her head. 'Hellava hard, Hennitjie.'

'Anyway,' she added – carefully testing the strength of the much-repaired spine of the biology book and then tucking it back into the satchel – 'I guess we'd better get moving or the books'll get wet.'

She laced Hennie's boots to the satchel, slung it over her shoulder, lifted Hennie on to the pony's back and, with a loud 'Gi-yip,' vaulted up herself and they were away. Waves of wind rattled through the maize, bent the long grass double and roared in Hennie's ears. Intusi's hard hooves thumped, her powerful shoulders and lungs working like a great engine. Hennie grasped the mane and turned the pony firmly towards the mountains, towards the storm: 'Fly, fly Intusi, faster,' she yelled, and yelled again as the pony responded and Mondi's arms tightened against the change of pace. The thunder, like the long low growling of a wild animal, was becoming more frequent.

But after too few minutes, Mondi was reaching round her, gentling the pony and directing them back towards the rutted track to the farmhouse. As they slowed, Hennie felt a few great wet drops against her face.

The storm broke as they reached the yard. Sheets of water whooshed over them, and they were soaked in a second. Mondi leapt off the pony to drop the satchel, boots dangling, in the shelter of the stoep. Then she carried Hennie across, ran Intusi to the stable and sprinted back. They must rush to put back Hennie's boot and caliper; Hennie hated her father to see her without her boots on. So far, nobody had noticed their arrival.

Then came the hail, making the crash of a thousand drums on the tin roof. Hailstones ricocheting in the yard spattered them as they struggled with the boot. The gushing rain, mist closing in and steam rising from the warm earth walled off the outside world. Mondi's shiny black hair was full of hailstones, like a cherry tree in blossom. Pebbles of ice and great drops of water fell into Hennie's lap as Mondi leant over her, wiping the water off her foot, cold and curled up like a sleeping mouse, pressing the foot back into its iron and leather prison. She paid no attention when Hennie winced, but firmly buckled the caliper over the khaki sock and fastened the laces.

Then she stood back, water streaming down her body and over her beautiful feet, and waited while Hennie struggled out of the chair and began to limp up and down – the first steps were always a bit more sore.

'I reckon Pa's home, man,' she said, putting off the moment of opening the door. She pictured her father standing at the window, arms folded tight across his rifle, peering into the mist in case cattle thieves should try to use the storm for cover.

'Reckon so,' replied Mondi, 'with all this rain.' Unsmiling as ever, she picked up the satchel and held it out for Hennie.

Hennie took a deep breath. She could feel her blood pounding in time with the hail. She looked at Mondi and saw her as other people did – a scrawny black girl with no shoes wearing a soaking-wet ragged vest and skirt made out of mealbags. Water was dripping off her chin, nose and ears and she made no attempt to wipe it away. Hennie was suddenly enraged at the stupidity of it all.

'Ag, that useless thing,' she said, lunging at the satchel, 'I don't want that stupid thing. You take it away.'

'What? This?' Mondi gave a brief joyless laugh. 'Are you going mad or something?'

'Ja, keep it – *A Christmas Carol* and the English dictionary and the biology and the maths set, all of it.'

Now Mondi was shocked. She stepped back, and Hennie felt herself swamped with a terrible need to cry. She stood hard on her bad foot, bringing on the sharp and familiar pain that always brought her to her senses.

Her tone changed. 'Yes, please keep it Mondi,' she said. 'Go on. It's what I want. I'll tell them I lost it in the storm. But keep it at the mission or they'll say you stole it.'

'Ag, no man. You know you can't. It doesn't belong to you; it belongs to the baas. I know there isn't any money to buy another one. You can't do such a thing. It'd be a sin.'

'What do I need it for?' cried Hennie. 'I'm going to be a bankrupt farmer, like my pa. He can't speak English. He can't read novels. What use is it for me to be different? Hey?' and, after a pause, 'Go on Mondi, I want you to take it.'

'Ag, no man,' repeated Mondi, 'you don't have to try to be a farmer. You could maybe even be a schoolteacher one day. Ag no, no, never.' But Mondi's voice suddenly broke, giving away her excitement. Recognizing the signal, they both burst into a laugh at the same moment.

It was done.

Hennie nodded brusquely and went into the house.

'Hennitjie, is it you?' Her mother's voice from the kitchen rose above the sound of the hail, thinning now. 'Come here and dry out by the stove. You'll get a terrible cold. They should've kept you at school.'

'What d'ya mean Ma?,' boomed her father's voice, 'They don't keep other children at school when there's a few drops of rain. The girl won't melt; you're turning her into a damn sissy.'

Hennie's left shoulder felt oddly light, as if, satchel-less, it was lifting up into the air. 'Coming ma,' she said.

But she didn't go directly. She peered through the mosquito netting, to see Mondi take off her tattered vest, wrap the satchel against the rain as if it was a living baby, and let herself out into the mist.

A Sunrise on the Veld

Doris Lessing

Every night that winter he said aloud into the dark of the pillow: Half-past four! Half-past four! till he felt his brain had gripped the words and held them fast. Then he fell asleep at once, as if a shutter had fallen; and lay with his face turned to the clock so that he could see it first thing when he woke.

It was half-past four to the minute, every morning. Triumphantly pressing down the alarm knob of the clock, which the dark half of his mind had outwitted, remaining vigilant all night and counting the hours as he lay relaxed in sleep, he huddled down for a last warm moment under the clothes, playing with the idea of lying abed for this once only. But he played with it for the fun of knowing that it was a weakness that he could defeat without effort; just as he set the alarm each night for the delight of the moment when he awoke and stretched his limbs, feeling the muscles tighten, and thought: Even my brain – even that! I can control every part of myself.

Luxury of warm rested body, with the arms and legs and fingers waiting like soldiers for a word of command! Joy of knowing that the precious hours were given to sleep voluntarily! – for he had once stayed awake three nights running, to prove that he could, and then worked all day, refusing even to admit that he was tired; and now sleep seemed to him a servant to be commanded and refused.

The boy stretched his frame full-length, touching the wall at his head with his hands, and the bed foot with his toes; then he sprung out, like a fish leaping from water. And it was cold, cold.

He always dressed rapidly, so as to try and conserve his night-warmth till the sun rose two hours later; but by the time he had on his clothes his hands were numbed and he could scarcely hold his shoes. These he could not put on for fear of waking his parents, who never came to know how early he rose.

As soon as he stepped over the lintel, the flesh of his soles contracted on the chill earth, and his legs began to ache with cold. It was night: the stars were glittering, the trees standing black and still. He looked for signs of day, for the greying of the edge of a stone, or a lightening in the sky where the sun would rise, but there was nothing yet. Alert as an animal he crept past the dangerous window, standing poised with his hand on the sill for one proudly fastidious moment, looking in at the stuffy blackness of the room where his parents lay.

Feeling for the grass edge of the path with his toes, he reached inside another window further along the wall, where his gun had been set in readiness the night before. The steel was icy, and numbed fingers slipped along it, so that he had to hold it in the crook of his arm for safety. Then he tiptoed to the room where the dogs slept, and was fearful that they might have been tempted to go before him; but they were waiting, their haunches crouched in reluctance at the cold, but ears and swinging tails greeting the gun ecstatically. His warning undertone kept them secret and silent till the house was a hundred yards back: then they bolted off into the bush, yelping excitedly. The boy imagined his parents turning in their beds and muttering: Those dogs again! before they were dragged back in sleep; and he smiled scornfully. He always looked back over

his shoulder at the house before he passed a wall of
trees that shut it from sight. It looked so low and small,
crouching there under a tall and brilliant sky. Then he
turned his back on it, and on the frowsting sleepers,
and forgot them.

He would have to hurry. Before the light grew strong
he must be four miles away; and already a tint of green
stood in the hollow of a leaf, and the air smelled of
morning and the stars were dimming.

He slung the shoes over his shoulder, *veld skoen**
that were crinkled and hard with the dews of a
hundred mornings. They would be necessary when the
ground became too hot to bear. Now he felt the chilled
dust push up between his toes, and he let the muscles
of his feet spread and settle into the shape of the earth;
and he thought: I could walk a hundred miles on feet
like these! I could walk all day and never tire!

He was walking swiftly through the dark tunnel of
foliage that in daytime was a road. The dogs were
invisibly ranging the lower travelways of the bush, and
he heard them panting. Sometimes he felt a cold
muzzle on his leg before they were off again, scouting
for a trail to follow. They were not trained, but
free-running companions of the hunt, who often tired
of the long stalk before the final shots, and went off on
their own pleasure. Soon he could see them, small and
wild-looking in a wild strange light, now that the bush
stood trembling on the verge of colour, waiting for the
sun to paint earth and grass afresh.

The grass stood to his shoulders; and the trees were
showering a faint silvery rain. He was soaked; his
whole body was clenched in a steady shiver.

---

* *veld skoen*: shoes made from rawhide

Once he bent to the road that was newly scored with animals' trails, and regretfully straightened, reminding himself that the pleasure of tracking must wait till another day.

He began to run along the edge of a field, noting jerkily how it was filmed over with fresh spiderweb, so that the long reaches of great black clods seemed netted in glistening grey. He was using the steady lope he had learned by watching the natives, the run that is a dropping of the weight of the body from one foot to the next in a slow balancing movement that never tires, nor shortens the breath; and he felt the blood pulsing down his legs and along his arms, and the exultation and pride of body mounted in him till he was shutting his teeth hard against a violent desire to shout his triumph.

Soon he had left the cultivated part of the farm. Behind him the bush was low and black. In front was a long *vlei**, acres of long pale grass that sent back a hollowing gleam of light to a satiny sky. Near him thick swathes of grass were bent with the weight of water, and diamond drops sparkled on each frond.

The first bird woke at his feet and at once a flock of them sprang into the air calling shrilly that day had come; and suddenly, behind him, the bush woke into song, and he could hear the guinea fowl calling far ahead of him. That meant they would now be sailing down from their trees into thick grass, and it was for them he had come: he was too late. But he did not mind. He forgot he had come to shoot. He set his legs wide, and balanced from foot to foot, and swung his gun up and down in both hands horizontally, in a kind

---

* *vlei*: low-lying ground in which a lake forms in the rainy
    season

of improvised exercise, and let his head sink back till it was pillowed in his neck muscles, and watched how above him small rosy clouds floated in a lake of gold.

Suddenly it all rose in him: it was unbearable. He leapt up into the air, shouting and yelling wild, unrecognizable noises. Then he began to run, not carefully as he had before, but madly, like a wild thing. He was clean crazy, yelling mad with the joy of living and a superfluity of youth. He rushed down that vlei under a tumult of crimson and gold, while all the birds of the world sang about him. He ran in great leaping strides, and shouted as he ran, feeling his body rise into the crisp rushing air and fall back surely on to sure feet; and thought briefly, not believing that such a thing could happen to him, that he could break his ankle any moment, in this thick tangled grass. He cleared bushes like a duiker*, leaped over rocks; and finally came to a dead stop at a place where the ground fell abruptly away below him to the river. It had been a two-mile-long dash through waist-high growth, and he was breathing hoarsely and could no longer sing. But he poised on a rock and looked down at stretches of water that gleamed through stooping trees, and thought suddenly, I am fifteen! Fifteen! The words came new to him; so that he kept repeating them wonderingly, with swelling excitement; and he felt the years of his life with his hands, as it were, as if he were counting marbles, each one hard and separate and compact, each one a wonderful shining thing. That was what he was; fifteen years of this rich soil, and this slow-moving water, and air that smelt like a challenge whether it was warm and sultry at noon, or as brisk as cold water, like it was now.

*   duiker: a small antelope

There was nothing he couldn't do, nothing! A vision came to him, as he stood there, like when a child hears the word 'eternity' and tries to understand it, and time takes possession of the mind. He felt his life ahead of him as a great and wonderful thing, something that was his; and he said aloud, with the blood rising to his head: all the great men of the world have been as I am now, and there is nothing I can't become, nothing I can't do; there is no country in the world I cannot make part of myself, if I choose. I contain the world. I can make of it what I want. If I choose, I can change everything that is going to happen: it depends on me, and what I decide now.

The urgency, and the truth and the courage of what his voice was saying exulted him so that he began to sing again, at the top of his voice, and the sound went echoing down the river gorge. He stopped for the echo, and sang again: stopped and shouted. That was what he was! he sang, if he chose; and the world had to answer him.

And for minutes he stood there, shouting and singing and waiting for the lovely eddying sound of the echo; so that his own new strong thoughts came back and washed round his head, as if someone were answering him and encouraging him; till the gorge was full of soft voices clashing back and forth from rock to rock over the river. And then it seemed as if there was a new voice. He listened, puzzled, for it was not his own. Soon he was leaning forward, all his nerves alert, quite still: somewhere close to him there was a noise that was no joyful bird, nor tinkle of falling water, nor ponderous movement of cattle.

There it was again. In the deep morning hush that held his future and his past, was a sound of pain, and repeated over and over: it was a kind of shortened scream, as if someone, something, had no breath to scream. He came to himself, looked about him, and called for the dogs. They did not appear: they had gone off on their own business, and he was alone. Now he was clean sober, all the madness gone. His heart beating fast, because of that frightened screaming, he stepped carefully off the rock and went towards a belt of trees. He was moving cautiously, for not so long ago he had seen a leopard in just this spot.

At the edge of the trees he stopped and peered, holding his gun ready; he advanced, looking steadily about him, his eyes narrowed. Then, all at once, in the middle of a step, he faltered, and his face was puzzled. He shook his head impatiently, as if he doubted his own sight.

There, between two trees, against a background of gaunt black rocks, was a figure from a dream, a strange beast that was horned and drunken-legged, but like something he had never even imagined. It seemed to be ragged. It looked like a small buck that had black ragged tufts of fur standing up irregularly all over it, with patches of raw flesh beneath . . . but the patches of rawness were disappearing under moving black and came again elsewhere; and all the time the creature screamed, in small gasping screams, and leaped drunkenly from side to side, as if it were blind.

Then the boy understood: it *was* a buck. He ran closer, and again stood still, stopped by a new fear. Around him the grass was whispering and alive. He looked wildly about, and then down. The ground was black with ants, great energetic ants that took no notice of him, but hurried and scurried towards that fighting shape, like glistening black water flowing through the grass.

And, as he drew in his breath and pity and terror seized him, the beast fell and the screaming stopped. Now he could hear nothing but one bird singing, and the sound of the rustling, whispering ants.

He peered over at the writhing blackness that jerked convulsively with the jerking nerves. It grew quieter. There were small twitches from the mass that still looked vaguely like the shape of a small animal.

It came into his mind that he should shoot it and end its pain; and he raised the gun. Then he lowered it again. The buck could no longer feel; its fighting was a mechanical protest of the nerves. But it was not that that made him put down the gun. It was a swelling feeling of rage and misery and protest that expressed itself in the thought: if I had not come it would have died like this: so why should I interfere? All over the bush things like this happen; they happen all the time; this is how life goes on, by living things dying in anguish. He gripped the gun between his knees and felt in his own limbs the myriad swarming pain of the twitching animal that could no longer feel, and set his teeth, and said over and over again under his breath: I can't stop it. I can't stop it. There is nothing I can do.

He was glad that the buck was unconscious and had gone past suffering so that he did not have to make a decision to kill it even when he was feeling with his whole body: this is what happens, this is how things work.

It was right – that was what he was feeling. *It was right and nothing could alter it.*

The knowledge of fatality, of what has to be, had gripped him and for the first time in his life; and he was left unable to make any movement of brain or body, except to say: 'Yes, yes. That is what living is.' It had entered his flesh and his bones and grown into the furthest corners of his brain and would never leave him. And at that moment he could not have performed the smallest action of mercy, knowing as he did, having lived on it all his life, the vast, unalterable, cruel veld, where at any moment one might stumble over a skull or crush the skeleton of some small creature.

Suffering, sick and angry, but also grimly satisfied with his new stoicism, he stood there leaning on his rifle, and watched the seething black mound grow smaller. At his feet, now, were ants trickling back with pink fragments in their mouths, and there was a fresh acid smell in his nostrils. He sternly controlled the uselessly convulsing muscles of his empty stomach, and reminded himself: the ants must eat too! At the same time he found that the tears were streaming down his face, and his clothes were soaked with the sweat of that other creature's pain.

The shape had grown small. Now it looked like nothing recognizable. He did not know how long it was before he saw the blackness thin, and bits of white showed through, shining in the sun – yes, there was the sun, just up, glowing over the rocks. Why, the whole thing could not have taken longer than a few minutes.

He began to swear, as if the shortness of the time was in itself unbearable, using the words he had heard his father say. He strode forward, crushing ants with each step, and brushing them off his clothes, till he stood above the skeleton, which lay sprawled under a small bush. It was clean picked. It might have been lying there years, save that on the white bone were pink fragments of gristle. About the bone ants were ebbing away, their pincers full of meat.

The boy looked at them, big black ugly insects. A few were standing and gazing up at him with small glittering eyes.

'Go away!' he said to the ants, very coldly. 'I am not for you – not just yet, at any rate. Go away.' And he fancied that the ants turned and went away.

He bent over the bones and touched the sockets in the skull; that was where the eyes were, he thought incredulously, remembering the liquid dark eyes of a buck. And then he bent the slim foreleg bone, swinging it horizontally in his palm.

That morning, perhaps an hour ago, this small creature had been stepping proud and free through the bush, feeling the chill on its hide even as he himself had done, exhilarated by it. Proudly stepping the earth, tossing its horns, frisking a pretty white tail, it had sniffed the cold morning air. Walking like kings and conquerors it had moved through this free-held bush, where each blade of grass grew for it alone, and where the river ran pure sparkling water for its slaking.

And then – what had happened? Such a swift surefooted thing could surely not be trapped by a swarm of ants?

The boy bent curiously to the skeleton. Then he saw that the back leg that lay uppermost and strained out in the tension of death, was snapped midway in the thigh, so that broken bones jutted over each other uselessly. So that was it! Limping into the ant-masses it could not escape, once it had sensed the danger. Yes, but how had the leg been broken? Had it fallen, perhaps? Impossible, a buck was too light and graceful. Had some jealous rival horned it?

What could possibly have happened? Perhaps some natives had thrown stones at it, as they do, trying to kill it for meat, and had broken its leg. Yes, that must be it.

Even as he imagined the crowd of running, shouting natives, and the flying stones, and the leaping buck, another picture came into his mind. He saw himself, on any one of these bright ringing mornings, drunk with excitement, taking a snapshot at some half-seen buck. He saw himself with the sun lowered, wondering whether he had missed or not; and thinking at last that it was late, and he wanted his breakfast, and it was not worthwhile to track miles after an animal that would very likely get away from him in any case.

For a moment he would not face it. He was a small boy again, kicking sulkily at the skeleton, hanging its head, refusing to accept the responsibility.

Then he straightened up, and looked down at the bones with an odd expression of dismay, all the anger gone out of him. His mind went quite empty: all around him he could see trickles of ants disappearing into the grass. The whispering noise was faint and dry, like the rustling of cast snakeskin.

At last he picked up his gun and walked homewards. He was telling himself half defiantly that he wanted his breakfast. He was telling himself that it was getting very hot, much too hot to be out roaming the bush.

Really, he was tired. He walked heavily, not looking where he put his feet. When he came within sight of his home he stopped, knitting his brows. There was something he had to think out. The death of that small animal was a thing that concerned him, and he was by no means finished with it. It lay at the back of his mind uncomfortably.

Soon, the very next morning, he would get clear of everybody and go to the bush and think about it.

REVELATIONS

The Stolen Party

For discussion

1   Rosaura's mother refers to Luciana as 'that one'. What are your impressions of Luciana?

2   How does the author catch and keep the reader's interest? At what point is the climax of the story? Were you surprised?

For writing

3   Write an account of Rosaura's mother.

   - What kind of a person is she?
   - How does Rosaura feel about her?
   - How well does she understand Rosaura?
   - Look again at some of the things Rosaura's mother says. Why does she say them? In the light of what happened at the party, do they make sense?

4   There are two sides to every story. Write Senora Ines' account of the party. You could begin when Rosaura arrives, or you could start even earlier. In your account you should bring out her feelings towards Rosaura and the other children.

How Table Mountain Got Its Cloth

For discussion

5 What do you learn from the story about life in South Africa? How is it different from your society? How is it similar to your society?

6 The viewpoint of the author, Norman Silver, often comes across from the things that Basil says. What can you gather about the author's attitudes?

For writing

7 Structure refers to the ways different parts of a story fit together. Examine the structure of *How Table Mountain Got Its Cloth*. To do this, among other things you will need to:

- identify the three different stories within the main story
- show how the different stories are linked together by the characters
- explain how the beginning of the story links with the ending.

8 How does the author achieve humour in the story? Identify the parts of the story that make you smile, and try to explain why this happens. Some of the things you could consider are:

- the way people talk
- unlikely comparisons
- descriptions of people
- incongruous situations
- unexpected reactions
- children's jokes
- exaggeration.

Making comparisons
For discussion
9 Dolly and Rosaura react differently when offered money. Explain how they react, and try to account for the differences in their behaviour.

10 What examples of prejudice can you find in these stories?

For writing
11 Amos says, 'Nothing's as simple as it looks.' In what ways could this statement apply to the two stories? You could consider:

- Senora Ines' treatment of Rosaura
- Rosaura's enjoyment of the party
- the stories about Table Mountain
- Floyd and Dolly
- Amos himself.

12 Compare and contrast the characters and lifestyles of Rosaura and Basil.

Suggestions for imaginative writing
13 Choose a landmark with which you are familiar. (It could be anything from a tree to a factory chimney.) Make up a story about how it came to be there.

14 'There are two sides to every story.' Write a story based on this theme.

15 Basil says that you can never guess from a person's shoes what that person is really like. Write about a character, real or imaginary, to whom this comment could apply.

ROOTS

Beneath the Baobab

For discussion

1   Why does Tyrone Brown describe himself as being
    a *mzungu* (white person) with a black skin?

2   What did you learn about the Lunda tribe? Did
    any things surprise you? Examine their good and
    bad points, making comparisons where possible
    with your own society.

For writing

3   Chief Kinombwe says to Tyrone Brown: 'We
    might even find that we are not so different after
    all, though our customs and traditions would have
    us believe otherwise.' Compare and contrast the
    two men, looking at the differences which arise
    because of the men's natures and characters and
    those which arise because of their cultures and
    upbringing.

4   How is tension created and maintained in the
    story? To help you, among other things you could
    look for:

    • pivotal points in the structure of the story
    • areas of conflict between characters
    • unexpected twists in the plot
    • changes in pace
    • the creation of atmosphere
    • the role of the baobab itself.

Footprints

For discussion

5 In what ways does the weather help both the plot and the creation of atmosphere in the story?

6 Examine the significance of the Sydney Opera House, shells and the sails of sailing boats.

For writing

7 Write an account of the similarities between Benny and Bennelong. Include in your comparison an examination of their strengths and weaknesses, and their relationships with other people. Could they have been the same person at different periods in time?

8 'Caught between cultures.' What essential differences can you find between the way the aboriginals lived in Bennelong's time and Benny's way of life in the culture of Australia today?

Making comparisons

For discussion

9 Both stories are about fallen trees. Why is this significant?

10 In both stories, reality is suspended for a while. How plausible is this? Does it affect your understanding and enjoyment of the stories?

For writing

11 Compare the lives of Bennelong and Chiti. Rather than merely narrating events, try also to reconstruct a lifestyle for each of them. Some hints and details can be found in the stories, but you will need to use ideas of your own to expand on these.

12 Assess the gains and losses which Benny and Tyrone Brown experience after their time-slip encounters.

Suggestions for imaginative writing

13 Create your own time-slip story, involving the felling of a tree, and the appearance of some unusual phenomena connecting the past with the present.

14 'Before and After.' Describe a place before and after a dramatic event occurs. This event could be natural, for example, a storm, or it could be caused by the activities of people.

15 Imagine it is fifty years time and you are a grandparent. Relate a piece of family history to your grandchildren.

MONEY MATTERS

Mr Sookhoo and the Carol Singers

For discussion

1   How does the use of dialect affect your understanding of the story? Would the story have been better without dialect or would something have been lost? Try reading some excerpts in standard English and some in a dialect which you know, to help you reach a decision.

2   What are your feelings about Mr Sookhoo?

For writing

3   The headmaster's opinion of Mr Sookhoo changes at various points in the story. Identify these points and say how he feels at each stage and why his opinion subsequently changes.

4   Tell the story from the point of view of Horace.

Cat Within

For discussion

5   Does the exorcist know what is in the jug? Give reasons for your answer.

6   What are the problems which the tenants of the ancient house in Vinayak Mudali Street complain about? Is there any justification for their complaints?

For writing

7   Write the story from the point of view of the cat, beginning when it is stalking a mouse and ending with its escape from the jug.

8   Imagine you are a journalist who arrives in the town shortly after the cat has escaped. Write a story about the event in a way which your readers will find interesting, remembering to include some comments from eyewitnesses.

Making comparisons

For discussion

9   Are there any morals or lessons to be learnt from these two stories?

10 How do the writers create humour in the stories? Which story did you think was funnier? Try to explain why.

For writing

11 In what ways are the lives of the people in the stories different from your own? Write about anything which you found interesting and unusual, and also give details of any of the things which you are glad you do not have to experience.

12 Both Mr Sookhoo and the shopkeeper take advantage of other people. Compare what they do and decide who you think has committed the more serious crime. You might like to include in your analysis a discussion of some of the following:

- the kind of people they are
- the environments in which they live
- their motives
- their behaviour towards others
- whether or not they deserve to be punished.

Suggestions for imaginative writing

13 Write a story about someone who plays a trick which misfires.

14 Using your imagination, or writing from experience, describe an eccentric character. You should try to include the following details:

- appearance
- mannerisms
- distinctive behaviour
- treatment of others
- speech
- interests and dislikes.

15 Write an account of an incident in which a creature, which could be as large as a horse, or as small as a fly, creates havoc.

ROUGH JUSTICE

The Martyr

For discussion

1 Why does Njoroge prefer working for someone like Mrs Smiles rather than someone like Mrs Hills? Does this surprise you?

2 Discuss the ways in which the ending links with the beginning of the story, and the irony of the situation.

For writing

3 Examine Njoroge's attitude to white people and to Mrs Hill in particular. Include in your discussion an examination of the possible reasons for his feelings, and say whether or not you agree with them.

4 What do you learn about life in Kenya at the time the story was written? Although you could briefly include some historical facts, you should concentrate on describing what life was like for different groups of people.

Naukar

For discussion

5 How would life have been different for Julia and Nilkant if they had been living in England instead of India?

6 What might the rickshaw-wallah be thinking at the end of the story?

For writing

7   Throughout the story, there are various sources of conflict between Julia and Nilkant. Identify these, and for each say with which character you are more in agreement.

8   What impressions do you get of Calcutta from this story? Show how Anya Sitaram effectively conveys the atmosphere of the city.

Making comparisons

For discussion

9   Throughout *Naukar*, Julia is referred to by her first, rather than her married, name. In *The Martyr,* however, we are never told Mrs Hills' first name. What impressions does this give you about the narrators of the stories? Does it affect your responses to the two women?

10   Both stories examine the attitudes of a female employer to a male servant. Why do you think this is? Could the stories have worked as well if the employers had been male and the servants female?

For writing

11   In *Naukar*, Julia thinks about the 'fragile co-existence of rich and poor'. There are also two groups, rich and poor, in *The Martyr*. What are the similarities between the rich groups in each country and the poor groups in each country? In which country do you think the co-existence is more fragile?

12   'Home' to both Mrs Hills and Julia is England. Assess the ways in which they have adapted to the different cultures of Kenya and India.

Suggestions for imaginative writing

13 Write your own story, with the title 'Rough Justice', in which someone is wrongly accused of a crime.

14 Write a story in which two characters who experience the same event, interpret it differently. You could if you wish, construct the story as two separate accounts.

15 Using your imagination or writing from memory, describe an incident in which an intended good deed has the opposite result. Pay particular attention to the creation of character.

HEAT AND DUST

A Drink of Water

For discussion

1 What were the causes of Rannie's sickness?

2 Examine the relationship between Rannie, Manko and Sunny. How does this account for what happens in the story?

For writing

3 Identify the various emotions which Manko experiences during the course of the story. Avoid narrating the story, concentrating instead on what Manko feels at each stage.

4 Continue the story after the drought has passed and the rains are falling regularly. Pay particular attention to how the villagers might react to and treat the Rampersads.

Looking for a Rain God

For discussion

5 'Tragedy was in the air.' Was it a tragedy, or just a very sad story?

6 We learn more about the two little girls, Neo and Boseyong, than we do about their mother. How does this affect our responses to the story?

For writing

7 'It was really the two women who caused the deaths of the little girls.' How far do you consider this statement to be true?

8   Write two separate speeches to be presented during the trial of the old man Mokgoboja, and Ramadi. One speech should be the summing up for the defence and the other should be the summing up for the prosecution.

Making comparisons
For discussion
9   In both stories people have to cope not only with hostile environments but also with the greed and selfishness of others. Which people benefit from the severity of the situation?

10   The treatment of death in a story is never easy. Examine the ways in which Samuel Selvon and Bessie Head tackle this subject, and the effectiveness of their treatment.

For writing
11   How do the authors convey the atmosphere of the drought-ridden countryside, and the despair it creates in individuals?

12   Compare and contrast the rituals and beliefs presented in the two stories. You could include a discussion of some or all of the following:

- the nature of the offerings
- who the offerings are made to
- the ironies of the situations which arise after the rituals
- the people who make the decisions
- the feelings of other people involved
- benefits and losses to the community as a whole and to individuals
- your own responses and reactions.

Suggestions for imaginative writing

13 Write a story with the ending '… and then it rained'. You can set your story anywhere. It does not have to be in a rural area as it is in these two stories.

14 Almost every society has its own superstitions, and has developed rituals to cope with these. Describe a superstition with which you are familiar, explaining what might happen if the obligatory rituals were not observed. You could include some examples from personal experience if you wish.

15 Imagine there has been no running water in your community for a week. Write a newspaper report describing the situation. As well as giving examples of hardship and resourcefulness, show how some people have benefited from the situation. You should also include comments from local residents, as well as from employees and directors of the water company.

BETRAYAL

Country Lovers
For discussion
1   Paulus says, 'I feel like killing myself.' Why does he feel like this?

2   Why does Thebedi change her version of events in court?

For writing
3   Nadine Gordimer, talking about the characters in her stories, once said: 'They are what they are because their lives are regulated and their mores (social customs and moral principles) formed by the political situation.'[*] To what extent are the actions and responses of characters in *Country Lovers* controlled by the culture of the society in which they live?

4   Would the story have been more, or less powerful if Thebedi's baby had not been killed? You will need to examine how the death affects the following aspects of the story:

- the development of character
- the plot and structure of the story
- the author's viewpoint and intentions
- your own responses.

[*]   *London Magazine 1965*

The Bamboo Blind

For discussion

5 After hoping no one will want to marry her, why does Razia change her mind when she hears about Razak?

6 What are your impressions of Hasina, Razak's eldest sister? Why do you think she stares so much at Razia?

For writing

7 Razak tell Razia, 'In many ways it is just like Lucknow', when explaining about life in Britain. What are the similarities about Razia's life in the two places? Are there any differences?

8 Who is responsible for the 'betrayal' in this story? Is it Razia's family in Lucknow, Razak, Razia's in-laws in Manchester, the culture to which Razia belongs, Razia herself, or a mixture of some or all of these?

Everyday Use

For discussion

9 How does the author prepare the reader for the arrival of Dee? Is there anything which surprises you when she does arrive?

10 In the earlier part of the story, Maggie's mother has a dry, caustic humour. How is this achieved, and why is it effective? Towards the end of the story this humour disappears. In what ways is this significant?

For writing

11 In what ways do Maggie and Dee differ in their approach to, and appreciation of, their cultural heritage?

12 Trace the reasons why Maggie's mother finally refuses to give Dee the quilts.

Making comparisons

For discussion

13 Identify and comment on the causes of conflict in the stories.

14 In which of the stories do you feel that the author is most sympathetic to the characters she has created?

For writing

15 Examine the strengths and weaknesses of Paulus, Razak and Hakim-a-barber; Thebedi, Razia and Maggie. Given the circumstances which they face, who, in your opinion, has the strongest character, and who has the weakest?

16 How effective are the openings (first few paragraphs) of the stories in preparing the reader for what happens later? You will need to look at the following aspects of each opening:

- setting
- atmosphere
- character creation
- plot development
- tone and style.

Suggestions for imaginative writing

17 Create your own story on the theme of 'Betrayal'.

18 Write about an object which is very important to you. It could, for example, be a family heirloom, a gift or souvenir, or something from your childhood. As well as describing the object, also explain how it came to be in your possession, and the nature of its significance.

19 Write an account of how a tense family situation develops because of a misunderstanding between members of different generations. You could, if you wish, set out your account in the form of a playscript.

CHANGING LIFESTYLES

The All-American Slurp
For discussion
1 In your opinion, which member of the Lin family finds it easiest to adapt to the new lifestyle? Why do you think this is?

2 At which meal was Lensey Namioka most embarrassed? How would you have felt and reacted?

For writing
3 Imagine you are Meg. Write a series of diary entries, including in each one some comments about events you have shared with Lensey Namioka, and your feelings about her.

4 Write an account of the ways in which the Lin family have to adapt to the American way of life. You should include in your account a discussion of:

- eating habits
- speaking the language
- dress and appearance
- sport and leisure activities
- attitudes towards education
- their achievements.

The Empty Amulet

For discussion

5 Paul Bowles does not use speech marks in this story. How do you feel about this? Does the absence of speech marks make the story difficult to understand? Are there any advantages?

6 What is ironic about Habiba doing her embroidery with a modern German machine?

7 Was Moumen right or wrong to deceive Habiba with the false baraka?

For writing

8 Compare Habiba's life before marriage with her life after marriage.

9 Habiba and Moumen eventually get divorced. Write two letters: one from Habiba to her father saying why she no longer wishes to stay married to Moumen, and one from Moumen to Habiba's father saying why he no longer wishes to be married to Habiba.

After the two letters write a paragraph stating which letter Habiba's father is more likely to understand, and give your reasons.

Making comparisons

For discussion

10 What did you learn about the roles of men and women in the two stories?

11 What were your first impressions of :
    a) Meg
    b) Habiba's friends?

Did these impressions change at all during the course of each story?

For writing

12 Write an essay comparing the ways in which the two stories are written, ending with a conclusion about which story you found most effective. Answering the following questions and giving reasons for your answers will help you to structure your essay:

- Which story did you enjoy most?
- Which story gave you more to think about?
- Does having a third person rather than a first person narrator make a difference to the story?
- In which story did you find the characters more convincing?
- Were you happy with the endings, or did you wish they could have been different?
- Do you think the humour, or absence of it, was appropriate?
- Which story better enabled you to learn about other people's customs?
- Which story gained most from the use of dialogue?

13 Examine the ways in which Lensey Namioka and Habiba adapt to their new environments. You should include in your discussion your opinions about who you think is more successful, and why.

Suggestion for imaginative writing

14 Write a story in which you face problems trying to remain an individual when friends are trying to persuade you to conform to their ideas. Do you stand firm against the pressures, or do you give in?

15 Imagine you are going to live in another part of your country, or even in another country altogether. Write an account of the adjustments you would expect to have to make, and say how you think you would cope with the most difficult ones.

16 Every culture has its own rituals about eating. Describe in detail a family meal in your house. Try to explain why certain procedures are followed.

FACING THE FUTURE

Mondi

For discussion

1   What opinions does Martinus van Rensberg have about education?

2   Why is the story called *Mondi* rather than *Hennie*?

For writing

3   'Despite the differences in their lifestyles and background, Hennie and Mondi have much in common.' How far do you agree with this statement?

4   What impressions do you get of the author's views about:

   • black people
   • white people
   • black/white relationships in South Africa?

A Sunrise on the Veld

For discussion

5   At one point the author says about the boy: 'There was nothing he couldn't do.' A little later the boy is thinking: 'There is nothing I can do.' What happened to bring about the changes in the boy's thoughts? What were your reactions to the changes?

6   Do you attach any significance to the fact that the boy has no name?

For writing

7 Select six adjectives to describe the boy. Write an extended paragraph about each adjective, explaining when and how it applies to the boy.

8 Compare the boy's environment with your own, including in your discussion an assessment of those features, from both his environment and your own, that you do not like and those which you do like.

Making comparisons

For discussion

9 What does freedom mean to Mondi and Hennie in *Mondi* and the boy in *A Sunrise on the Veld*?

10 Imagine Hennie, Mondi and the boy in ten years time. Who is likely to have experienced the greatest change in their life?

For writing

11 Examine the relevance of the settings in the two stories. You could consider, among other things, some of the following:

- importance of the land
- symbolism of the elements
- friendly/hostile environments
- effect of physical environment on character
- creation of atmosphere
- differences and similarities between the two stories
- importance for the development of plot.

12 Compare the ways in which Hennie and the boy reach their decisions.

Suggestions for imaginative writing

13 Describe a place that is special to you. Try to create the appropriate atmosphere in words and images so that the setting is vivid and interesting for the reader.

14 Create a piece of original writing on the subject of 'Freedom', tackling the subject in any way you wish. Some possibilities you could consider are:

- short story
- poem
- travel article
- feature article for a magazine
- speech
- playscript
- series of related anecdotes and thoughts
- informal letter to a friend
- formal letter to an organization.

15 'A Day That Changed My Life.' Choose a day from your childhood to which this title could apply. Explain what happened and how you changed. Although it is often easier to recollect bad experiences rather than good times, you should try to include some positive experiences in your account.

Heinemann
New Windmills

Alan Gibbons Chicken
Graham Greene The Third Man and The Fallen Idol; Brighton Rock
Thomas Hardy The Withered Arm and Other Wessex Tales
L P Hartley The Go-Between
Ernest Hemmingway The Old Man and the Sea; A Farewell to Arms
Nigel Hinton Getting Free; Buddy; Buddy's Song
Anne Holm I Am David
Janni Howker Badger on the Barge; Isaac Campion; Martin Farrell
Jennifer Johnston Shadows on Our Skin
Toeckey Jones Go Well, Stay Well
Geraldine Kaye Comfort Herself; A Breath of Fresh Air
Clive King Me and My Million
Dick King-Smith The Sheep-Pig
Daniel Keyes Flowers for Algernon
Elizabeth Laird Red Sky in the Morning; Kiss the Dust
D H Lawrence The Fox and The Virgin and the Gypsy;
Selected Tales
Harper Lee To Kill a Mockingbird
Ursula Le Guin A Wizard of Earthsea
Julius Lester Basketball Game
C Day Lewis The Otterbury Incident
David Line Run for Your Life
Joan Lingard Across the Barricades; Into Exile; The Clearance;
The File on Fraulein Berg
Robin Lister The Odyssey
Penelope Lively The Ghost of Thomas Kempe
Jack London The Call of the Wild; White Fang
Bernard Mac Laverty Cal; The Best of Bernard Mac Laverty
Margaret Mahy The Haunting
Jan Mark Do You Read Me? (Eight Short Stories)
James Vance Marshall Walkabout
W Somerset Maughan The Kite and Other Stories
Ian McEwan The Daydreamer; A Child in Time
Pat Moon The Spying Game
Michael Morpurgo Waiting for Anya; My Friend Walter;
The War of Jenkins' Ear
Bill Naughton The Goalkeeper's Revenge
New Windmill A Charles Dickens Selection
New Windmill Book of Classic Short Stories
New Windmill Book of Nineteenth Century Short Stories

How many have you read?